W
CRITSER

Critser, David.

Border town law

W

BORDER TOWN LAW

BORDER TOWN LAW

David Critser

Walker and Company
New York

First published in the United States of America in 1994 by Walker Publishing Company, Inc.

Published simultaneously in Canada by Thomas Allen & Sons Canada, Limited, Markham, Ontario

Library of Congress Cataloging-in-Publication Data
Critser, David.
Border town law / David Critser.
p. cm.
ISBN 0-8027-1278-9
I. Title.
PS3553.R534B67 1994
813'.54—dc20   93-11750
CIP

Printed in the United States of America

2 4 6 8 10 9 7 5 3 1

For my father, who was a cowboy at heart.

BORDER TOWN LAW

CHAPTER 1

JOE TRENTO SAT his horse for over ten minutes, taking in the scene below. He was on the top of a gently sloping foothill that provided a tremendous view of a desert expanse. From Joe's vantage point, the land below appeared smooth and flat . . . even pretty. But he knew it was a blistering, rock-strewn plain, filled with rattlers and prickly pear.

This knowledge accounted in part for the young man's procrastination. Beyond the horizon, in the dip of an often dry river valley, was Joe's destination, the town of San Martin, New Mexico. Getting there meant a four-hour ride through the searing midday sun.

He usually planned his journey so as to cross the basin during the early-morning cool, but this time circumstances had dictated a different schedule. Finally, he let out a deep sigh, touched his heels to his roan, and started down the slope.

As he rode, he planned what he should do. Upon arriving in town, he would go immediately to the marshal's office. If the lawman wasn't there, Joe could leave a message or possibly inquire as to his whereabouts. Joe wanted to finish his business that very afternoon, before it grew too late. He didn't want to spend the night in San Martin, or else he would find himself crossing the basin during midday again.

Suddenly, the gelding raised its head and flicked its ears backward. Joe knew that it had heard something besides the usual desert sounds. He reined up, pulled Blue halfway around, and looked back.

1

Coming over the same knoll upon which he had just sat were five riders, moving at a gallop. From what Joe could make out, they appeared to be ordinary cowhands. They continued toward him, and he was surprised that they apparently intended to gallop their mounts straight into the searing desert, as if upon some urgent mission. He waited to let them pass.

The men were about fifty yards away when Joe began to feel that something was wrong. All five seemed to stare intently in his direction, and they continued at a flat-out run. Two men had picked lariats from their saddles and appeared prepared to throw. Puzzled, Joe instinctively reached down and loosened the large Colt resting in his tied-down holster.

They were almost upon him. The two with lariats suddenly threw; the lassos shot through the air and hovered over Joe and his horse. Joe spurred the gelding viciously, and it bolted forward with a lunge. At the same time, he ducked, hoping to slip under the ropes. The first sailed harmlessly over the rump of Blue, but the second caught and jerked him from the saddle.

Joe twisted to land on his left side. The man who had missed was galloping toward him, noose hanging low. Although his shoulders were pinned to his sides, Joe's lower arms were still free. His hand flashed and he fired. Instantly, he covered the other man and fired again. So quick were his movements that his two shots sounded like one.

Both shots were good. The first man tumbled backward, a .45 slug in his shoulder. The second let out a grunt as the bullet struck his arm. He dropped his rope to grasp the wound. The other three, surprised by Joe's quick reaction, hesitated a moment.

Joe leapt to his feet, struggling to regain his balance. Two of the remaining men drew revolvers; the other pulled and leveled a carbine.

"You're a dead man, mister," called the youngest, "unless you drop it now!"

Joe looked around. One man was rising slowly, holding his shoulder and swearing. The other, still clutching his arm, had also drawn and leveled a six-gun. Slowly, Joe Trento let his own weapon drop to the ground.

"Get your hands up and turn around!" said the same cowboy. "You handle a six-gun real good, mister, but you can't outgun five men. Move an inch and I'll put a bullet in you!"

"What the hell is this all about?" Joe asked. He turned slowly and raised his hands.

"Stranger, you may think you had a pretty clever plan," said an older man, the one with the carbine, "but you made just one mistake too many."

"I don't know what you're talking about."

"I think you do. Ev, tie his hands. Chico, catch his horse. We'll take him in to the marshal."

"That's where I was headed!" cried Joe, anger rising in his voice. "I was going to see the marshal myself. I don't know who you fellows are lookin' for, but you've got the wrong man!"

"That's quite a coincidence—you goin' to see the marshal too. Well, you'll see him now," said the one Joe had hit in the shoulder. He was a big, bearish-looking man, with long dark hair and a bushy beard. He glared angrily as his wound was tended to.

Joe straightened up and stared back. He was just as tall as the other man, and a bit more broad in the shoulders. His hat had spilled off and sandy hair had fallen onto his brow. He had a worn, rugged look, the result of living in the wild for too many years.

The wounded man held Joe's gaze for a moment, then looked away.

"You-all best have a good reason for this," Joe said. "I don't take to bein' run down like a stray calf."

"We've got a helluva reason, mister, and you know it," said the old fellow.

After Joe's hands had been tied and the wounded seen to, the Mexican brought Joe's horse over, then stooped down, grabbed Joe's gun, and stuck it in his own belt.

"Let's mount up," said the white-haired man. "The sooner we get to town, the sooner we get this done with."

Joe was shoved up onto his horse. He saw no reason to speak further. This bunch was obviously convinced that he was some outlaw or thief. He'd just have to wait until they saw Josh Parker, the town marshal. Parker knew him from Joe's previous visits to San Martin. Parker would put a stop to this nonsense.

They rode in silence, save for an occasional grunt or low curse from one of the wounded men. Joe wondered who they could possibly think he was. He knew few people in the area, and had not been associated with any individuals or activities that could make him suspect of wrongdoing.

He had recently purchased a sizable ranch in the mountains above the desert, an impressive purchase for a man of his years. He already called it a ranch, although at this point it was merely a chunk of wild, rugged land. Joe had partnered with an old hand, Al Grundy. Weary from many dusty years as a drover and wrangler, Grundy hoped to live out his days in relative peace and stability.

Joe's parents had been farmers in Mississippi until his father was killed in the war. Joe was sixteen at the time. When his mother passed away a year later, the boy decided to head for Texas, where he'd heard that a man could make a great deal of money rounding up and branding the wild cattle roaming the hills and ravines.

But after paying his parents' debts and settling various affairs, Joe found that he had little cash and few possessions of value left over. The trip to Texas required the use of much of these funds, and once at his destination, Joe realized that he lacked both a large enough grubstake and sufficient knowledge to carry out his plans. The young man wandered through Houston and further south, hoping to stumble across an opportunity to enter the cattle business. His only prospects, however, were as a hired hand with the larger outfits. These were either wealthy cattle companies and large ranches, or sometimes small groups of men with the same aspirations as Joe. But those men were experienced cowboys with money for horses and equipment. Joe was almost penniless, and had no experience whatsoever in the Texas backcountry, so he started out taking whatever jobs he could get.

Joe Trento enjoyed his life on the range and the hard work that came with it. He generally preferred the wilderness and the company of horses and cattle to the bright lights and music of the frontier towns. However, he had seen much of both worlds, and his friendly manner and skill with rope and six-gun had won him more than a few friends. And those who came to know him found that the easygoing cowboy was afraid of nothing, and could become a fearsome lightning bolt of an adversary when provoked. Oftentimes, even those who had just met the young man sensed this quality about him.

The group had covered over a mile, and still none of them had spoken. Joe Trento's attention was suddenly caught by the youth they called Chico. He had pulled the six-gun from his belt and was toying with it, bringing the piece to half-cock and spinning the cylinder.

"Careful with that gun, boy," Joe said. "It's a hair trigger. You drop it, and it's liable to shoot your pony in the belly."

"Relax, mister," replied the kid. "I'm just lookin'. Never seen a six-gun quite like this before."

"My advice is to unload it before you fool any further, but save the loads. I'll be wanting them back soon enough."

"You'll not be getting anything back, stranger," sneered

the man with the wounded arm. "If you don't hang within the week, you'll rot in jail the rest of your days."

Joe was startled at this information, but said nothing. He had assumed that the men had run him down as a suspected small-time outlaw—a petty thief of some sort. Being accused of a hanging offense was another matter, and Joe's concern deepened.

Chico hadn't quit examining the gun, but Joe noticed that he had removed the cartridges. It was an unusual piece, and Joe's favorite—a .45-caliber Colt Army, with special grips, a modified sear—or hair trigger—and a disfigured hammer spur, filed down bit by bit to hit Joe's hand in a certain way during a fast draw.

Joe remembered buying the Colt several years ago, at the end of a drive in Abilene. He purchased it new from one of the gunsmiths in town and immediately ordered the modifications. He had been working trail drives up from Texas for three years and had learned much about horses, longhorns, and guns.

Joe found that there were generally three types of cowboys as far as revolvers were concerned. One group owned no pistol at all, either because they couldn't afford one or because they didn't believe in the practicality of them. Instead, these men usually possessed Winchester or Henry rifles. Another group—the majority—carried a revolver in a plain holster while on the range. They realized that a cowboy often needed to draw a weapon quickly and shoot with one hand, usually at a rattler or a rustler, but perhaps at a marauding Indian or puma.

The third group consisted of only a few men on Joe's first drives. They carried their love of revolvers and gunplay to an extreme. Each possessed fine, large-caliber weapons and carried them in low-slung, cutaway rigs. They made an art of quick draw and fancy, rapid-fire shooting.

Joe had been drawn to them, not due at first to his interest in guns, but rather to his desire to make friends.

The lonely youngster was anxious to be part of a group, and the gunslingers were the closest to Joe's age. They were also fairly fun loving and outgoing.

Joe Trento found that his new friends were also happy to teach him about guns and shooting. Except for an occasional small stampede, a river crossing, or some similar excitement, most trail drives were routine and boring events. Any interesting conversation was a welcome diversion during the day. During the evenings, the cowboys would let Joe handle their revolvers—each had several—while they took turns explaining the particular characteristics of each one.

The oldest of these men, Thaddeus Corbett, owned four revolvers. He loaned young Joe a Navy model, and on many evenings the two would crunch through the buffalo grass until they were several hundred yards from the herd. Then they would shoot. Joe had a natural ability, and marksmanship fascinated him immediately.

On one particular evening Joe had had even better than usual success hitting pieces of wood tossed into the air by Corbett. After quickly firing five times and hitting his mark five times, Joe turned to see his friend staring at him with a startled look.

"You're all right with that Navy, boy," Corbett had said. Joe still remembered the long, peculiar stare.

With his hands bound tightly behind his back, and his hat mashed down over his head, Joe was having a sweaty, uncomfortable ride into town. He tried several times to bend and wipe the perspiration from his eyes, but he accomplished little. Therefore, he was relieved when at last the group topped a small rise and looked down upon the town of San Martin, a mile or so off.

CHAPTER 2

THEY APPROACHED FROM the north and headed down the main street. San Martin was a typical New Mexico town, consisting mostly of wooden buildings, several with false fronts. Board sidewalks lined the street in the center of town, and a dozen or so side streets intersected the main one. Some of the structures were of adobe, especially at the edge of the settlement.

It wasn't uncommon to see ranch hands ride into town at any time of day. San Martin boasted three saloons in addition to the mercantile, livery, bank, and hotel. A few hired hands, and quite a few drifters from the surrounding country, often visited the town after payday or a long period on the range.

At first, the people on the street that morning only glanced at the riders. Then, as they noticed that Joe Trento's hands were tied, they began to talk excitedly.

The six men rode on to an adobe and stone building near the middle of town, which housed the jail and marshal's office. The five dismounted, and Trento was pulled roughly from his gelding. He landed hard in the dusty street.

With his hands bound, Joe could only raise himself slowly into a sitting position. While doing this, he heard the sound of boots approaching down the wooden walk, then a voice.

"Morning, Cal, boys. What the heck's going on here?"

Joe twisted his head around. He could see Josh Parker standing in front of the jail.

"Here's the feller that killed Shorty," said the old man.

"We went back to the place where the stock was run off and followed the trail. Seems the beeves spooked and scattered when he tried to move them across the Big Sandy. I figure he spotted us coming down, so he gave up on the stock and run for it. Prob'ly would've headed clear to Mexico. We seen what he was up to and run him down."

The marshal stepped into the street and stood over Joe. "You're the boy that bought land up north of Big Sandy." He turned to the others. "This boy's been in town a couple of times. He and a partner are settin' up a spread ten or fifteen miles north."

"If he's going into the cattle business," said the big man, sneering, "he's rustlin' the cattle to do it."

The marshal glanced around at all of the men. "Looks like you all have had a rough morning. He give you some trouble, Spence?"

"Got me in the shoulder, and Fergus over there too. He's a gunslinger, Marshal. He beat the five of us, and him on the ground with a rope around him."

Joe finally spoke up. "Marshal, you know me. I've been to town three times, buying supplies. I was on my way in today when this bunch ran me down. I don't know what they're talking about."

"What's your name again, son?"

"Trento. Joe Trento."

"That's right. Joe, what were you coming for? You were just here not more than a week ago."

"I was coming to see you. I'm having trouble with rustlers myself." Snickers arose from Spence and Fergus and a short laugh from the young man named Everett. "I came straight down from my place," continued Joe. "Started before daybreak. I'd just gotten out of the hills when they came along."

"Why were you cutting across? Why didn't you stay in the hills and come around?"

A small valley, a fingerlike extension of the desert,

protruded northward into the mountains. Joe's ranch was north of the valley; San Martin was on the western edge, at a place where mountains melted into sand and cacti.

"Like you said, Marshal. I've just been to town a week ago. I can't spend all my time riding to San Martin and back. I took the shortest trail possible."

"Well, Joe, you seemed like a regular enough fellow before, but I've got to admit, I really don't know much about you—"

"That's right," chimed in the old man, "and how did a feller his age get hisself any land around these parts? Where in the hell did he come from? I say he's a killer and a thief!"

The marshal turned to the old man. "Cal, didn't you say your girl Millie saw Shorty get shot down?"

"Well . . . yes," said Cal. "Last night she took a ride out to where Shorty was huntin' strays. Wasn't far from the house—over in some tangled-up woods by the river. She's the one who rode back and told us."

"Then maybe she could tell us if Joe here is the killer."

"Well, I suppose, Josh, but hell, we just about caught him red-handed. I mean, we trailed him right down out of the hills where the strays were."

"A judge would want more evidence than that," Parker said.

"Judge, hell!" bellowed Spence. "He should be strung up right now! We've no need of a judge!"

The marshal ignored him. "You better arrange to bring her down, Cal." The lawman turned to Joe. "Sorry, son, but it looks like I'm going to have to lock you up."

"That's crazy!" cried Joe. "You can't jail me based on a story like this!"

"I'm afraid I can, and I have to, Joe," replied the marshal.

Joe stood unbelievingly, his face flushed with anger. Just a few hours ago he had been heading in to report some rustling . . . the law was on his side then. The marshal would've treated him like any respected townsperson. Now he was treated as a thief and a murderer!

"This'll be a lesson to any other cattle thieves thinking about doing their stealin' around here," said Spence. "I'll enjoy seein' you swing from a rope, mister."

Joe shot an icy stare at the man, but said nothing.

"You all just worry about gettin' Millie down here," said Parker. "I can't hold him forever on suspicion. Chico, you tie his horse up right here. I'll have Billy tend to it later. And I suppose one of you has his gun. I'll take it." Chico dismounted and reluctantly handed over the Colt. Then he led the blue roan forward and tied it to the rail.

"You lock him up good, Josh," said the old man. "He's a son of a bitch, and he'll run if'n he gets the chance." The five men turned their mounts and trotted off down Main Street.

The marshal motioned Joe toward the jailhouse. Joe stepped across the wooden walk and pushed open the door.

The front room of the little building contained a desk and several chairs, and served as the lawman's office. A small door led to a cell in the rear of the edifice. The marshal nudged him toward the cell.

"Sorry, son, but this is the best way. You're safer in here than out there with the Milsteads running about. You really got them all afire by winging Spence and Fergus. How'd you manage that, anyway?"

"I'm not inclined to sit by and be drug all over the country," Joe replied. "I'd have gotten a few more, but I was hoping they'd take a good look and see that they had the wrong man."

Marshal Parker frowned. "Well . . . you must be good, like they said. Both Spence and Fergus are fast themselves. And Spence ain't exactly an even-tempered soul, case you haven't noticed. Not the type of feller you want to be making enemies of."

Joe walked through the cell door, and the bars clanged shut behind him. He turned and faced the lawman. "Let's get one thing straight, Marshal. Those men rode out of the hills and ran me down. I don't aim to make an enemy of anyone. They've got the wrong man. Seems you've already got me tried and judged—and that doesn't sit well." Joe tried to keep the anger out of his voice, but his sudden movement and big size startled Parker a bit. The lawman took a step back.

"It may not sit well. In fact, I'm sure it don't. But I'm marshal here and I've got certain things to look to. You were in a fix out there, if you didn't notice. Where'd you be if I'd just turned you loose? Think on that a minute."

Joe thought a minute. "Who are those men anyway?"

"That was Calvert Milstead and his sons—except for Chico. There's a couple of women up at their place, too. The whole bunch moved in about five years ago and settled right north of here. You're about ten, fifteen miles from their place."

"Don't seem much like stockmen to me."

The marshal leaned a shoulder against the adobe wall and began fishing around in his vest pocket.

"They ain't. Not that Milstead ain't had a good enough opportunity. That high country has plenty enough grass. A man who is willing to work should have no problem up there. Cal and his bunch though, they ain't exactly the hard-workin' type. They trailed a few hundred head in from Texas—where they got 'em I'm not sure—and then just let 'em run wild, seems to me. Let 'em roam up there for over a year at a time. There's nothing necessarily wrong with that, of course, only most outfits have men riding the range periodically, keeping an eye on where the stock is, running them down to good pasture when they get too far up, that sort of thing." The lawman found his pipe and tobacco and paused a moment to light up.

"A lot of work for five men," remarked Joe.

"That it is. Milstead doesn't have it in him to hire on men and run a proper outfit. He's a bit of a drunk, if you ask me, and his boys are followin' in his footsteps. They spend a helluva lot of time here in San Martin, drinking and dealing poker hands over at the Red Dawn, or sometimes at the North Star."

The marshal puffed vigorously for a moment, filling the little room with smoke. "Anyway, after the first two years, old Cal figured out that his herd was spread out all over the range north of here, some dead from the winters, or stolen, or lost. So he and the boys finally started ridin' the high country, lookin' for all the beeves they could find. Several small outfits up north came up missing stock. Of course, no one has come up with actual proof of anything, but it seems that Milstead considers the whole northern part of the territory to be his range. I've heard rumors— brag talk, you know—that the Milsteads would shoot up any outfit that tried to start up in the area."

"It's a cheap land, Marshal. Why doesn't he buy the range that he needs?"

"That, I don't know. Like I said, he's no businessman. Besides, Cal's type figures the range is free land, open to the first man that kills off the savages and settles in."

"This figures right in, Marshal!" cried Joe. "Milstead has prob'ly had some stock drift east and disappear into the canyons back there, so he's blaming me. Hell, sounds like they're more'n likely responsible for my missing cows. And from what you say, he's just lookin' for an excuse to run me out!"

"Well, trouble is, there is actually some evidence of rustling from Calvert's herd too. Not much . . . probably drifters or Indians. But it's my job to take it seriously, whether I like it or not. I said it before. You struck me as an honest man, Joe, but for all I know maybe you really were after some of Cal's herd.

"Last night Cal rode in to tell me about the shooting. From what he said, Millie just about rode in on it. Apparently she saw the killer standing right next to the body—right next to Shorty's fire. The gunman shot in her direction, then jumped on his horse and was off. That's the story, anyway. The girl should have gotten a good look, with the fire and all. And from the time Cal gave me, there should've still been some light left.

"If this is all just blow, like you say, maybe they won't even bring the girl in. Maybe they'll just drop it . . . or maybe the girl will see right off that you're not the one, and you'll be free to go. Meantime, I figure you're best off in here."

"Was Shorty one of Cal's boys too?"

"No, I believe he met up with the Milsteads somewheres in Texas. He seemed to be a decent feller to me. Probably was lookin' for work, and Cal saw that he'd make a good hand, so he took him on. You've seen him around. He was always in town picking up whatever supplies and such they needed. Short feller, bushy beard, but no mustache. Peculiar looking."

Joe indeed recalled seeing such a man once or twice.

"The Mexican boy, Chico," the marshal added, "isn't his either, of course. He came with them too. No ma or pa I'd guess."

The lawman puffed thoughtfully for a moment. "There ain't a lot of solid citizens here in San Martin yet, especially men who can handle a gun. Got to admit, I'd have a tough time keeping the Milsteads in line if they really wanted to take things into their own hands. Pretty hard cases. I'm inclined to humor 'em, so long as they don't break no laws here in town."

"Humor them at my expense, you mean."

"Maybe—but remember, if you weren't locked up in here, you'd be dealing with those five out there."

"I'll take my chances."

"Can't let you, Joe. I think it's best we wait till Millie gets here." The marshal turned and started toward the door. "I'll send my deputy, Billy, by shortly—and we'll see to your horse." The marshal left, the heavy door clanging shut behind him.

CHAPTER 3

JOE MADE A quick survey of the stone cell. Opposite the door was a small barred window, set high up. A bunk lined one wall, and a washstand with water jug and washbasin stood nearby. He poured some water into the basin and cleansed his face, hands, and forearms. Now that the excitement was over, he began to feel the bruises and aches that had resulted from the morning's events. He sat down slowly on the bunk and rested his face in his hands.

Something didn't seem right about the whole mess. No reasonable men would have run him down and accused him on such meager evidence. It was a ridiculous charge. Amazingly, however, it seemed to be holding up.

They were definitely a hard bunch. Joe could tell from the way they rode and roped and dressed. He recognized the same traits in this group that he had seen in many desperadoes before.

Joe agreed with the marshal in one respect. Cal and his clan didn't seem serious about running a cattle operation. Joe had seen the type before. They made their living by bullying and threatening everyone else in the area, rather than by hard work. With no competition for the range, the boys could spend most of their time drinking and carousing around San Martin and the other small towns within riding distance. And with little effort, they might be able to round up and market a large herd within a few years.

The key to such a plan, Joe realized, would be to eliminate any competition. As far as he knew, his was the only other outfit nearby.

The big wooden door creaked, and Joe looked up to see a tall young man step through.

"Howdy," said the newcomer, grinning broadly. "I'm Billy Heywood, Parker's deputy." He stepped up to the bars.

"Howdy," said Joe.

"Marshal told me about it. Looks like you're goin' to be our guest. I doubt the Milsteads will be back in till morning. I'll be bringing your bedroll and some grub later on."

Joe let out a groan. "This is crazy! I came in to report rustlers, not to be jailed as one myself!"

The deputy shook his head slowly, but continued to grin. "Sorry, but I wouldn't worry too much. That Milstea clan is particular about the range up there. What hap pened to Shorty, I don't know, but I figure they went o the warpath, spotted you comin' along, and figured yo were the one."

"I've been settled in for more'n two months now," Jo said, "and I've been to town a lot of times. Does that soun like a drifting rustler to you?"

"No, it don't." Heywood rubbed his chin and looke thoughtful. "And I remember you in town before, buying at the mercantile. Hopefully, the girl will clear you . . . or mebbe they'll just drop the whole thing, like the marshal says, and not even show. That's the way they are. Meantime, you're best off in here."

Joe shook his head in disgust, walked back to the bunk, and lay down.

"Well I've got work to do," said Heywood. "We took care of your horse. Nice roan. I'll be back later with some vittles." The deputy left.

Joe spent the afternoon lying on the bunk. He tried to sleep, but was too upset. There was much work to do up at his place. He had been reluctant to even spend a day

coming to town; now he was wasting at least two, and he
hadn't even begun to solve the problem of his own rustlers.

The marshal was in and out during the course of the
afternoon, accompanied several times by merchants and
citizens, each conducting some business or other.

Heywood returned late in the day. He carried a plate of
food from the hotel and pulled up a chair while Joe ate.
The deputy still wore his good-natured grin, and Joe
began to enjoy the young lawman's company. This time
neither one brought up the subject of Joe's troubles;
instead, the talk turned to ranching, the surrounding
country, horses, and firearms.

With three saloons, a hotel, and other establishments,
San Martin was a place to visit and attracted its share of
drifters, prospectors, and cowboys. Nevertheless, it could
be a quiet place when the men were busy and no live'
visitors were in town. Shortly after Heywood left, Jos
Parker stopped back in to work at his desk.

"Cal and his boys left town right quick today," he com
mented. "They ought to have gotten back to their place a
a reasonable hour, so I expect they'll get an early star
tomorrow."

"Hope so, Marshal."

Parker cleaned up his desk a little more. He told Joe
that, being a quiet night and all, he'd just lock up, make
his rounds, and head home for the night. The thick door
thudded shut once more, and Joe Trento was left in almost
total darkness. In spite of his busy, anxious mind, his
weary muscles gradually relaxed as he lay on the cot. He
felt himself sink deeper into the straw mattress, and in a
moment he was asleep.

In the morning, Heywood arrived first and made coffee
on a small stove. He had passed a cup to Joe and was
preparing to seat himself outside of the prisoner's cell
when the two men heard the sounds of horses and a

buckboard. As Joe and the deputy watched, the door was thrown open and in strode Spence Milstead, big as a grizzly and looking mean.

"Where's the marshal?" he demanded, glancing around the office.

"Not in yet," said Heywood. "Should be here any minute, though."

The door opened again, and the rest of the clan entered. Cal Milstead brought up the rear, herding two girls in front of him. They both appeared to be in their late teens, but that's where the similarity ended. The one in front, the smaller of the two, walked with her head down, staring at the floor. A mop of thick black hair hung along each side of her face, and she wore a plain, well-worn, white dress.

Her companion was a more polished-looking young woman and carried herself well. Although young, she had a sophisticated look about her. Joe was admiring her pretty face and long auburn hair when Cal spoke up.

"Parker ain't in yet? It's getting on to eight o'clock! Bad enough we have to ride an extra thirty—"

"Here I am, Cal," said the marshal, stepping in. "And don't fret. We'll let Millie take a look at Trento here and you can be on your way in five minutes." The marshal walked toward the cell. "Morning, Millie. Morning, Elizabeth."

"Good morning, Marshal," said the taller girl.

"Now, Millie, if you'll just step a little closer, we can get this over with."

The smaller girl stepped forward timidly. Her companion followed, placing a comforting hand on her shoulder. Millie glanced quickly up at Joe, then returned her gaze to the floor.

"This here's the fellow you saw the other night, ain't he Millie?" said Fergus Milstead.

"Sure as hell is!" yelled Spence, stepping forward. "Why we oughta—"

"That's enough!" shouted the marshal. "Cal, I'll do the questioning here, and nobody else. You keep these boys in line, or the bunch of you can ride out right now."

"Keep your mouths shut," Cal said to the boys.

The marshal continued. "Now, Millie, you understand the seriousness of the situation here, don't you?"

"Yes, Marshal," said the girl.

"If you were a witness to a shooting, you could make the difference between life and death for this man. You understand?"

"Yes, sir."

"Fine. Now I want you to take another look at Joe here. Take all the time you need. Then tell me if this is the man you saw shoot Shorty two nights ago."

The girl looked up for three or four seconds, then glanced away again. Joe's eyes met those of her pretty companion. She held his gaze for several seconds, then looked away also.

"Millie," said Parker, "is this the man you saw the other night?"

The girl glanced at Spence and Everett. She stared at her feet again.

"Millie, you have to answer. Is this the man you saw?"

The girl stood frozen, not looking up. "Yes, Marshal . . . it's him."

"Marshal—!" Joe began, too astonished to continue.

"I knew it!" yelled Fergus triumphantly, shaking a fist at Joe. Then he winced and grabbed his wounded arm.

"Josh," said the old man, "I see no call for a judge. We 'bout caught him red-handed, and now we've got a witness."

"Well, now . . ."

"Millie," spoke up Elizabeth, "it was near dark when you saw the shooting. Were you able to see the man very well?"

"Elizabeth, shut up!" yelled Cal.

"Excuse me, Uncle. I just thought we should be sure."

"We are sure! Damn sure! She said this is the man. Josh, he's a killer and a rustler! He should hang!"

A chill shot down Joe's spine. This was getting out of hand. "Marshal, this is crazy! My partner is back at my place; he can tell you I was in camp two nights ago."

"Well, that would help some," said the lawman, "but he's your partner, so 'course he'd say that."

"And she's his daughter!" Joe shot back. "Is her word any better?"

"Josh, why don't you just hand him over to us right now?" said the old man. "The boys and me will find a stout tree down by the creek and take care of everything. He's a stranger here, remember, and folks'd have no problem at all with the marshal takin' care of a murdering stranger. Hell, neither would a circuit judge, from what I've seen."

"Cal, you know me better. I appreciate you all riding in today and bringing the girl, but the point of having the law is so these sorts of things can be handled in a certain way—a fair way. I'll be contacting the U.S. marshal about all this. You'll have to wait."

"The hell we will!" bellowed Spence. "We'll take him right now!"

"Right!" said Everett. "You're just a town lawman, not a federal marshal. You can't stop us from seeing justice done!" Everett had been sitting on a bench against the wall, but he jumped up now and stood next to Spence. The two wore Colt revolvers, strapped down in well-worn holsters. The brothers looked big, dirty, and mean.

Joe Trento surveyed the group. Fergus Milstead and Chico stood over by the desk, looking tense. Cal, Josh Parker, and the girls remained in front of the cell.

Parker glared at Spence. A boot scraped and all eyes shifted to see Billy step away from the opposite wall. He raised himself up to his full height and stood next to the marshal. He hitched his gun belt a bit higher up on his hips. His grin was gone, replaced by a stern, pale stare.

"I'll say it one more time," said Josh Parker. "Justice will be done. But it'll be done when we get a curcuit judge or a federal man in here. Now clear out!"

The brothers stared at the lawmen for a long moment. Suddenly, Spence gave a low curse, turned, and stomped out of the office. Everett shot a poisonous stare at Joe, then turned and followed.

"You have it your way, Josh," said Cal Milstead, his face flushed with anger, "but I spent last night burying one of my men up there in the hills. I won't forget that you kept this one from what he deserves." He shoved his hat onto his head and turned to go, motioning for the girls to precede him. Fergus and Chico followed.

Marshal Josh Parker turned to Joe. "I hate to say it, son but Cal was right about the judge. He'll likely see thing the same as them."

"Marshal, can't you see what they're up to? They wan the range to themselves, so they can run their herd withou hiring on help or branding any stock. I'm interfering with their plans, so they set me up!"

"I've thought of all that, Joe," said the lawman, "but with the girl's statement, it doesn't look good for you. I'll have Billy ride up to your place tomorrow and bring in your partner. After that, it'll be up to a judge." The marshal donned his hat and left.

Heywood now turned to Joe. His grin had returned. "Looks like you're in quite a fix. I only half-expected them to show up with the girl. I was hoping they'd drop the whole thing and Josh'd let you ride."

"I can't believe it," said Joe. "Way things are going, I could be found guilty by some snake of a circuit judge based on that little girl's say-so . . . say, who was that other gal?"

Heywood's grin grew wider. "Cal's niece. Parents are

dead, I believe. She came out here with the rest of the clan."

"Wouldn't of guessed she'd be kin of theirs," said Joe. "She's about the prettiest thing I've seen since I left Mississippi."

"She's certainly pleasant to look at. And you're right, she isn't from the same mold as the rest. Too bad she's stuck up there with that bunch. Well, I've got work to do this mornin'. I'll be riding out to Gil Dennis's place this afternoon. He claims some reservation bucks are helping themselves to his crop now and then. I'll check back in before I leave town, though."

CHAPTER 4

ONCE AGAIN, JOE Trento found himself alone in the jail-house, with nothing to do except to grow even more angry and frustrated. The remainder of the morning was a repeat of the previous day. Parker came and went, chatted with passersby, and worked for a while cleaning and oiling an old saddle and an even older shotgun. Joe guessed that the marshal of a town such as San Martin was not paid much and probably had to make the best of this type of equipment. About noon, Joe began to hear occasional laughter and shouting from the saloon across the street. He asked Parker about it.

"It's Spence, Everett, and Fergus Milstead," Parker said. "They've been over there since this morning. Their pa and the girls and Chico rode out, but these three stayed. There's a faro dealer passing through, and also some cowhands from somewhere. That may have something to do with it."

Joe was not happy with this news. He was sure that the marshal and his deputy would do everything possible to keep the Milsteads at bay—after all, the two lawmen had already stared the clan down this morning. Nevertheless, there were apparently not many law-abiding men in town—at least not fighting men—other than Parker and Heywood, and the Milsteads consisted of five tough guns, plus any drinking and gambling buddies they could muster. Joe had seen similar situations before in many a small trail town, and the outcome was often deadly.

Heywood returned at noon with two plates, one for Joe and one for himself. But the marshal and deputy sat at the

24

desk and talked in low tones while Joe ate alone in his cell. Joe noticed that the two glanced often through the front window in the direction of the drinking hole across the street, from which could be heard ever louder and more frequent shouts and peals of drunken laughter.

Joe wondered why the marshal didn't make the Milsteads leave town, but he supposed they had not broken any laws by drinking across the street. He knew that sometimes the best way to handle a drunk was to let him drink his fill, especially if there was the possibility of a shoot-out.

The two lawmen must have decided that the group in the saloon posed no immediate threat. Heywood finished his meal and got up to leave.

"I've got a good ride ahead of me to Gil's place," he said. "If I get moving, I can be back in four, five hours . . . in time to help see those boys out of town." Heywood grinned his grin. Joe nodded in return.

"I've got to admit," said Joe, "they do make me a little nervous."

"They'll likely make a good deal of noise, nothing else," said the deputy. "I wouldn't get too worried about them." The deputy donned his hat and strode out of the office.

"Billy's right," added the marshal. "That bunch spends a day or two each week doing it up over there. Sometimes evenings. It bothers some of the folks here in town, but generally there's no trouble." The marshal shoved closed his desk drawers. "Well, I've got a missus keepin' my dinner warm. I'll lock you in—I should return in an hour or so."

The afternoon crawled along. The marshal returned, wrote at his desk awhile, left again. Joe Trento was familiar with the habits of small-town lawmen. Parker would spend his day stepping briefly into most of the town's business establishments, sitting in front of the hotel, visiting with folks on the street. The idea was to be visible to any of the rowdy cowboys; to remind them that there was a town marshal in San Martin. No doubt, he would make a show of being useful to the townsfolk. The citizens needed to feel that their constable was earning his monthly stipend.

Joe continued to hear occasional commotion from across the street. At one point, hearing galloping horses, he rose and peered through the front window.

From his limited vantage point, he could view only a small portion of the Red Dawn saloon, but he was able to see four cowboys halt their horses and dismount. They seemed to be in a festive mood; they laughed, clapping each other on the back, and went inside.

Whoops, shouts, and more laughter came from the saloon. Joe guessed that the newcomers were acquainted with the Milsteads or their buddies. He frowned, sat down on the bunk, and for a while, strained to make out the talking and shouting from across the street. The merrymaking was louder than before, but the young prisoner could not decipher the words.

Suddenly the saloon doors banged open and several sets of footsteps clomped hastily across the wooden boards. Joe rose in time to see two men jump onto their ponies and tear off. He caught a fragment of speech: "North Star, first . . ." Joe wasn't sure but he thought that was the name of another beer hall. Were these two making the rounds of the other watering holes in San Martin? If so, why?

Dusk approached and Heywood had not returned. Josh Parker had been in twice, briefly, and had seemed nervous. The carousing across the street continued, a half dozen more gamblers and loafers joining the crowd.

A few minutes before nightfall, Parker stuck his head in the door and announced that he was going home to supper. He'd bring a plate to the jailhouse for Joe later on.

Joe was lying on his bunk, listening to the noises and wondering when the marshal would return, when he heard a group emerge from the Red Dawn. They stood talking noisily on the sidewalk. Joe peered through the front window and caught a glimpse of Fergus Milstead; he could also make out the deep voice of Spence, bellowing something to the others. Several additional patrons of the saloon spilled through its bat-wing doors. Some of the group stumbled off the wooden walk and milled about in the street.

"Marshal will be back any minute," said a voice. "We'll make 'im hand the bastard over!" It sounded like Spence. The rest of the crowd murmured their approval.

A lynch mob. Joe's stomach suddenly felt as though he had swallowed a large stone. He couldn't comprehend how, within forty-eight hours, he had been transformed from a free, law-abiding man, to an accused murderer, jailed and facing a lynching!

Joe knew that the mob could easily overpower the lone marshal, then break into the jail if they wished. Once again, the anger rose in him . . . resentment at being caged like an animal and having his life threatened. He glanced around the cell, thinking. Suddenly the crowd was silent. Joe heard a lone pair of bootsteps on the boards.

"You boys ready to head out?" It was Josh Parker! "What's the commotion out here?"

Joe could not make out the sharp reply, but the crowd roared in approval. Joe did not like the sound of that roar . . . he had heard it before. He must act quickly. He threw the dusty mattress off the bunk and slid the bed frame away from the wall.

" . . . enough of this . . . judge . . . day after tomorrow." Joe caught a few of the marshal's comments over the hum of the angry mob. He slid the bed frame to the center of the cell and paused. The sun had completely set now; Joe could no longer identify the figures across the street.

"We said we'll take care of this, and we mean it!" Spence's voice. Another clamor from the crowd, the sound of many boot heels . . . a desperate shout . . . then gunshots!

Joe, who had been sitting on the bed frame, jumped up. He bent and grasped the structure with both hands, gave a tremendous heave, and lifted the iron frame overhead. He took a moment to balance it evenly between his broad shoulders, then aimed his giant projectile at the small barred window high up on the adobe wall. Joe took two quick steps, then lunged, thrusting the iron forward with all his might. The frame hit the bars with a loud clang. Joe lost his grip and the frame bounced off his shoulder and gashed his arm as it fell to the floor.

He quickly surveyed the damage. The bottom ends of the bars had almost broken loose from their settings! As Joe had hoped, the aged adobe was dry and crumbling.

Eager voices sounded outside the jailhouse door. Joe heard the rattle of keys as if someone were searching fo the right one. He heaved the bunk overhead again, swun it around, and lunged. As the frame fell to the floor, Jo peered through the darkness. His heart leapt when he sa' the gap created by the damaged bars.

Everett Milstead found the right key on his fourth try. A he pushed the door open, he was almost flattened by th others behind him, including his huge brother Spence, charging forward. Ev stumbled to keep from falling. He looked up to see the group of men standing silently in front of the cell. It took them a few seconds to inspect the dim interior.

"He's gone!" cried Spence

"Window's busted out!" said his buddy, Rio. "Look!"

Once again, Ev had to stumble out of the way as the group turned and rushed out.

Joe figured that his chances for escape were slim, even though he was now free from the jail. A lot depended upon acting quickly. He needed a horse . . . and a gun, if at all possible. The mob would know that he was most likely still in the area, and they would begin searching the streets and alleyways in the immediate vicinity.

He dashed down the alley alongside the jail and darted across the street. He knew the drunken mob would emerge momentarily from the jailhouse; nevertheless, he paused over the lifeless body of Josh Parker and snatched up the lawman's six-gun.

Joe sprinted down a narrow passage outside the Red Dawn, hearing the first of the angry shouts from the jail. He reached the rear of the saloon and turned north, racing along behind the buildings. He remembered that Blue had been led off in this direction, and he hoped to find the livery.

After gaining about fifty yards, Joe heard shouts behind him, and then a gunshot! He turned and saw that two cowboys had emerged from an alleyway and spotted him. There was no place to hide. If he continued to flee, he'd be shot in the back. Their guns remained drawn as they came toward him. It was hard to fire accurately in the poor light.

Joe stood still and let them approach. Three, four seconds passed . . . suddenly Joe whipped the gun from behind him and fanned the hammer. Both men crumpled. Joe turned and sprinted north.

The livery was at the end of town. Joe entered and found his horse. Saddle and bags had been thrown in a corner of the stall. He bridled the gelding and threw on the saddle, not bothering to cinch it tight. A teenage boy, apparently a stable hand, walked in and called to him. Joe spurred the roan, and the big horse lunged from the stall, the boy leaping to one side. Horse and rider bolted through the stable door and raced north into the desert.

Joe Trento felt that his best insurance against recapture was simply distance. The streets of San Martin had been fairly empty during his escape. Most of the citizenry had been home at their suppers, many for the evening, and the nightly saloon-goers had not yet begun to appear.

Someone would soon find the two Joe had shot, but would not know for certain which way he had gone. Neither would the stable boy be sure. Any serious pursuit would not be organized for at least a few minutes, especially considering the mob's drunken state.

Joe had been moving at a comfortable lope for several miles before he stopped in a small arroyo. He dismounted and cinched his saddle properly. Grabbing the saddle and bags, rather than escaping bareback, had been a smart move. There was a Winchester rifle in its boot, cartridges for both rifle and revolver in the saddlebags, and in a hidden pocket, several dollars in currency. Joe only wished that he had his own Colt, but this was back in the dead marshal's desk drawer.

He mounted and continued north. He thought of Al Grundy back up at the ranch . . . surely Al would be concerned about Joe by now. It occurred to him that Al may have even had some trouble with the Milsteads himself. Joe's first reaction was to turn his gelding northeastward and head to the ranch. He realized, however, that his pursuers would expect this and certainly search for him there. If the two of them were found by a "posse" of Milstead's group, Al and Joe both would be killed.

With the marshal dead, and no other law nearby, Deputy Billy Heywood would have a hard time of it. It was unlikely he would be able to face up to the Milsteads forcefully enough to establish proper law and order in the area.

Joe Trento was afraid that his dream of building his ranch were crumbling before his eyes. But he wasn't going to give up easily. He turned his mount, tapped his spurs to its flanks, and aimed for the mountains west of the San Martin valley.

CHAPTER 5

JOE TRENTO AND Thad Corbett rode together on a lot of cattle drives over the years. Joe got good enough with a gun that he soon no longer needed Corbett's coaching. Nevertheless, the two spent a lot of time together practicing their shooting out on the range or enjoying the nightlife when in town. Finally, though, Corbett quit cowboying. His reputation for handling a gun had grown in the Texas and Kansas trail towns through which they passed, and people began to seek out Corbett to provide certain services requiring a fast and confident gun. Often the need arose due to the weakness or even absence of the regular law. At other times the question of right and wrong was muddled, but an individual or group still felt the need for this kind of help.

Corbett found that the compensation he received for such work soon surpassed his salary as a drover. Besides, the new occupation caused him to neglect his company duties. Finally, he left the trail altogether.

For the most part, Corbett was hired simply to present himself at some locale where the citizenry was having trouble with local toughs, something similar to the current situation in San Martin. At other times, he would be part of a group recruited by one side or another of a local land dispute or similar grudge. Thad Corbett was astute enough to consider these latter jobs carefully, pondering the justification for the battle and on whose side he was to fight.

His lightning-fast draw and handsome, steely grin won Corbett an even more widespread reputation as a tough gun. As was the case with many gunfighters, he quickly amassed a large number of bitter enemies, as well as a great many challengers—young quick-draw artists seeking fame and a reputation.

Around the time Joe had almost built enough of a grubstake to buy his own place he began to hear rumors of Corbett's retirement. Some even said he had gone east. Others, Mexico. The confusion was cleared up one evening in west Texas when Thad Corbett himself suddenly rode out of the dark and stopped at the chuck wagon.

"I'll be dipped and rolled in shit! Would you look at this!" exclaimed Blackie Mahoney, squatting by the fire.

"Corbett!" cried another. "Heard you was dead!"

"At the moment, I don't feel much alive, boys," said Corbett. "How about a cup of that coffee for an old man?"

Thad had stories to tell, and the bored drovers gathered around like children to hear about the fights and the women and the towns. No, he said, he wasn't retiring. He was fat and sassy and living high.

Later, however, he confided to Joe Trento that there was some truth to the rumors.

"Joey, you know pretty well how it is when you wear a gun like we do. You and me, we've seen some times together when we've had to draw fast and shoot our way out of a tight spot. When you wear a six-gun, even a little old scrap in a saloon becomes serious instead of it being settled with fists, or a chair in the face."

Joe nodded. "Some folks seem to get riled up at the sight of a stranger with a six-gun. I've even left mine behind, a time or two."

"I don't blame you. Not a bit. Me, I'm doing all right . . . I'm well paid, and I'm good at what I do. Just seem to be a bit spooky lately. Too many people know who Thaddeus Corbett is. Most of them have it in their minds that a hired gun is a killer. They don't want you spending too much time in their town . . . after you've done your job, that is."

Thad's big frame and square face looked a little more gaunt than Joe remembered. His rusty hair was shaggy, longer than even any of the trail hands'.

"What you figure you'll do?" Joe asked.

"Find new territory . . . take a rest for a while. I've got money enough. Probably take more respectable jobs from now on—maybe even become a peace officer somewheres. Some little place without much action."

Corbett rode out the next morning, headed for the border. He had mentioned a few towns he thought would be enjoyable, but private.

Look west of Texas, he had advised Joe when the young man had said he wanted to start his own ranch. Gone were the days when one could find wild longhorns roaming the scrub hills. Soon, he reckoned, a man would not be able to run cattle across open range at all. It would be fenced into pieces, owned by the individual outfits. To be a cattleman, one would have to own a piece himself. And the latest talk was that the cheapest, best land around was further west.

Joe's thoughts were interrupted by a noticeable change in the land. He was rising out of the desert basin and into more mountainous terrain.

His mind was made up. He remembered that Corbett had talked in particular about a border town called Morelos. The Milsteads would not expect him to circle around as he was now doing, then head south to Mexico. With a little caution and some luck, Joe figured he could be miles south of town by daybreak, headed for Morelos.

The land rose gently for a mile, then turned into more broken country, with frequent outcroppings of rock. Joe stopped and dismounted. He left the horse ground-tied and made his way up the slope on foot. About fifty yards away was a chaotic pile of jagged stone and boulders. He circled behind and began to scale the rubble. The pile was as big as a house, and when Joe neared the top he crouched and peered over.

There was no moon, but an incredible blanket of stars illuminated the desert quite well. So breathtaking was the view, that Joe temporarily forgot his worries and spent several minutes in a sort of peaceful trance. Finally, an impatient nicker from Blue reminded him of his purpose. He scanned his backtrail more carefully, but saw no sign of trouble. He slid back down the heap, returned to the gelding, and moved out at a trot.

Dawn found Joe forty miles south of the town of San Martin, still moving at a trot. He would push the roan a little longer, as it was still quite cool. Soon, however, they would slow to a walk. They were out of the mountains now and well into another of the large, basinlike valleys that separated the ranges. He had less fear of the Milsteads as time went on; his concern now was water. Before leaving the hills, both man and horse had drunk at a small stream. This would have to suffice for the day. Joe was headed for a settlement called Maysville, and he expected to arrive after dark. It would be a thirsty day, but nothing to be alarmed over. The trouble would come if Joe miscalculated and missed the town. A second day in the heat without water could be fatal.

Joe's thoughts were heavy now, due largely to fatigue and hunger. His plight had begun to seem more and more ominous. He wished now that he'd never left home that day to report the sporadic rustling out at his place. As a cowboy and a Texas drover, Joe knew that some amount of stolen cattle was always part of the business. But he'd felt that he had better report the incident.

Now he was running across a scorching desert, toward a destination over a hundred miles from his place. And he was wanted by the law, not to mention a gang of cutthroats.

Before him lay the task of whipping the whole Milstead family while somehow proving his innocence. Joe also felt some obligation to help Billy Heywood, who had been kind to him. The deputy was now the sole representative of the law in the frontier town, and a lot of folks' futures—including Joe's—depended on a certain amount of law and order.

Joe also had his partner to consider. Al Grundy's life, as well as their investment in the ranch, was at stake.

For his part, Joe was counting on an old friendship with a man some considered to be an outlaw himself. Thad Corbett might not be in Morelos. Even if he were, he might not be willing to throw in with Joe against the Milsteads. After all, what chance would the two of them have against the gang?

The hopelessness of the situation gnawed at Joe's weary mind as he struggled to stay awake. He had heard talk about sleeping in the saddle before, but had never much believed it. Now he felt himself dozing off. There had been sufficient travelers to Maysville to produce the beginnings of a trail, which the gelding recognized and was able to follow. As dusk fell over the creosote-and-agave-scarred landscape, Joe perked up enough to view a crimson sunset. Then the blanket of stars appeared again, and tonight, a sliver of a moon. Joe, feeling confident that the horse would find the way, relaxed again.

Moments later, the young stockman was truly asleep in the saddle, his hands holding the reins upon the saddle horn; his chin resting upon his chest.

He awoke with a start. The blue roan had stopped. Joe peered through the darkness and was surprised to see the town of Maysville, twinkling in the desert, several hundred yards away. He heard faint music and laughter. It was fairly early in the evening, judging by the light. Maysville was a tiny, one-street town established near a stream that was dry much of the time. A few shacks and decrepit dwellings were scattered across the surrounding plain.

Originally a small Mexican settlement, the town survived as a New Mexico trading post for the desert Indians and white travelers—homesteaders heading for more fertile country, prospectors seeking new claims, an occasional drifter. Only a few ranches operated successfully within fifty miles of the town.

Maysville was a smaller version of San Martin—more adobe, sand instead of dust. As Joe rode into town, a commotion was coming from a cantina down the street. He stopped in front of the place and dismounted. He entered and took a small table close to the door.

A Mexican behind the bar was chatting with two others seated on stools. Toward the rear of the room were a number of tables occupied by three or four groups of cowboys, laughing and playing cards. Several heads turned to look at Joe, and one man made a low comment, eliciting a peal of laughter from his fellows.

Joe noticed two women drifting among the tables, chatting and laughing with the men. One was Mexican, the other, Anglo. The latter looked like an aging whore, although her figure was still fair. The Mexican girl was young, dark, and quite pretty. Two more men sat farther down the bar.

The Mexican bartender gave Joe a curious look. Joe was not surprised that his appearance out of nowhere, hatless and beaten-up, raised some eyebrows. The man walked around the bar and approached.

"¿Señor?"

"A beer, and something to eat," said Joe.

"We have only some beans left. It is late."

"Beans then," said Joe. "Plenty of beans." The Mexican began to turn, then hesitated. "I have money," Joe said, "and a horse and gear outside." Joe wasn't about to pay in advance, but the bartender was welcome to check and see that his customer was a man of substantial possessions, not a bum.

The man only nodded, however. *"Sí, señor."* He returned to the bar and spoke to one of the young men, who then disappeared into a back room.

Joe turned his attention to the party in the rear. He saw the young Mexican girl approach the bartender, who was drawing the beer. She spoke briefly, took the glass, and walked to Joe's table.

"Buenas noches." She smiled and set the glass down.

"Thank you." Joe immediately took a long drink.

"May I sit down?" asked the girl. Joe looked at her over the rim of his glass. "I do not like so much smoke and noise," she said, indicating the gambling tables that she had just left. She looked embarrassed. Joe nodded.

The girl sat. "You look very tired," she said. "You are traveling?"

"Yes, to Morelos."

Her eyes brightened. "I know Morelos. I have relatives there. I like Morelos very much."

"I have a friend in Morelos myself," Joe said, deciding to take a long shot. "Perhaps you've heard of him. Thad Corbett."

"Yes, of course!" replied the girl

CHAPTER 6

JOE CHOKED ON his beer in surprise.

The girl continued, "He comes here sometimes, to Maysville. He is very kind. He is your friend?"

"Yes. In fact, I'm going to Morelos to look him up. Do you know if he's living there?"

"Yes, I think so. He has been here two times, coming from Morelos, and once returning from the north. He talks of Morelos as though he lives there. One time he stopped some drunken men from beating my cousin Pablo and smashing bottles. Pablo is the one getting the beans."

As though on cue, Pablo Orazco banged through a door at the rear of the cantina and strode forth purposefully, a steaming plate held high. He set it in front of Joe with a short bow. The girl spoke to Pablo in Spanish. He broke into a grin and bowed a second time. "Yes," he said, "*Señor* Corbett is a friend. Is he well?"

"I don't know," said Joe. "I haven't seen him in about a year. I was on my way to look him up when I . . . had an accident." Pablo had been glancing at Joe's torn clothing and bruised face. "Listen, Pablo," Joe said, placing two coins on the table. "Is there someone who could see to my horse? Water, a few oats, and maybe a quick rubdown?"

"*Sí, señor*, we have a place in the back. But a special price for a friend of *Señor* Corbett." Pablo smiled and bowed again, taking only one of the coins. He marched off. Joe turned to the girl.

"What is your name, *señorita?*"

"Lupita. And yours?"

"Joe." He shoved the spoon into the beans. Not much of

38

a meal, but there was plenty of it, and they were steaming hot and very spicy.

"Sometimes *Señor* Rodriguez—that is him over there—rents rooms in the back," Lupita explained. "There are two. We have no hotel in Maysville. Will you stay here tonight?"

Joe wondered about the girl's occupation. The Anglo woman was almost certainly a prostitute. She was still hanging around the card tables, her arm draped over one of the men. But Joe figured that Lupita kept to waitressing. Otherwise, she wouldn't be spending so much time with a beat-up stranger like him.

"No," Joe said, "I'm moving on. Sort of in a rush to get to Morelos. Thanks anyway." He planned on sleeping some later on, but out in the desert somewhere, both in order to save money and to avoid detection by anyone still following.

"We used to have a hotel here," the girl said, "but it closed. Now—"

"Lupita!" It was one of the cardplayers. "Some reason you find our company unsatisfactory all of a sudden?" It was the same man who had made the comment when Joe first walked in. He wore the garb of a fancy Texas cowboy, including two black-handled, Colt peacemakers. They looked new.

Joe didn't like the man. He had a cockeyed grin on his flushed face, and his eyes were glazed—he looked like he'd been drinking for more than one day. Now he approached and stood between the two.

"Here I come, Bobby," said Lupita. She started to rise.

"Oh, no, no!" He pushed her back down into the chair. "I'll not break up your little party. Stay here with the boy. He looks like he could use a little female companionship . . . couldn't you there, boy?"

"I'm leaving," said Joe. The beans were about gone. He took a last swallow of beer and stood up.

"Hold on, boy," said the gambler. "Don't let me scare you off your little gal here. Seems to me, a feller man enough to pack a gun like that shouldn't spook so easy."

Here it comes, thought Joe. He was wearing the dead marshal's gun, which was plenty noticeable. Although Joe's looks were somewhat boyish, he was about the same age as the cowboy and a little bit bigger.

"Listen, *amigo*," said Joe, "I've got an appointment to keep. I'm headin' out of town directly." It was the truth. But the man blocked Joe's way.

"And I say—"

He got no further. Joe gripped the back of the chair he had been sitting on and swung it in a wide arc. The gambler wasn't too drunk to get his hands up in time. The man crumpled to the ground as the chair smashed across his face.

Instantly, Joe's gun was out and pointing at the back of the room. Several men had risen and started to draw.

"Forget it!" Joe blurted. "I'm leaving—I've got business to attend to elsewhere. I stopped for a meal, not trouble. But I warn you, anyone else who tries me will die."

The speed of Joe's draw had a sobering effect on the cardplayers. Those in the act of drawing slowly put their guns away and stepped back. The others shuffled their feet and glanced at one another.

Lupita sat stunned in her chair. The Mexicans stood quietly by the bar. The injured man groaned and bled on the dusty floor. Still pointing his gun, Joe threw more coins on the table and motioned Pablo over.

"Is my horse saddled?"

"*No, señor.* You asked me to rub him down."

"Throw the saddle on and bring him around, pronto."

"*Sí, señor.*" Pablo headed out the rear door.

"Sorry, *señorita*," Joe said to the girl. "I'll tell Corbett you all said howdy." Joe backed toward the front door, pistol still aimed at the group.

Once outside, he dashed around the corner and saw Pablo leading Blue toward him.

"Thanks, Pablo. Sorry about the chair. I left a little extra on the table." Joe took the reins from Pablo.

"It would be safer for you to come this way," Pablo said, leading Joe and Blue back behind the cantina toward a dry riverbed.

"Maybe you'd best get back and look after Lupita. Those fellows may be a bit riled at her."

"Do not worry about her. Rodriguez, he treats her like a daughter. The men don't go too far with her. And when we tell everyone that you are a friend of Corbett, they will leave us alone. They can see that you have experience, not like these *ladrones* around here. It will help Rodriguez to have friends like you and Corbett around. You must come back very soon."

The men and horse had slid down the gravelly slope to the dry wash. They could hear voices coming from the direction of the town.

"No," Pablo continued, "there is no one around here to face a *pistolero* like him. We have heard that he killed three men in Bad Axe. Also, he was a special deputy in Santiago, and—"

"Sorry, Pablo, I wish I could help but I've gotta ride." Joe mounted. He was nervous about the men in the saloon, although he hoped they'd be too intimidated to follow. The boozer he hit may have been the only real hard case; still, Joe was jumpy.

Pablo took off his sombrero and handed it up to Joe. "Take this, Joe. The valleys are very hot. You must have a hat."

He was right. "Thanks, Pablo." Joe flipped the big hat onto his head.

"Instead of following this wash," Pablo said, "you should ride west two miles. There is another river there, also dry. Follow it south, and it runs into a big arroyo where you will be safe for the night. There will be water too, if you dig. If the pistolero tries to find you, he will not think to look for you in that place."

"Thanks, Pablo."

"What is the rest of your name, Joe?"

"Trento—Joe Trento," Joe called back as he nudged the gelding into a trot.

Peering through the darkness, Pablo was able to make out the figure of Joe Trento as he cut up the bank of the dry wash, after traveling some distance, and headed out over the plain.

A few of the gamblers were now standing in front of the cantina. They watched Pablo as he came down the street, but said nothing. Pablo entered and went to the bar where Rodriguez, Lupita, and a Mexican named Miguel talked quietly. The rest of the place was empty, except for the Anglo woman and a single man sitting together in the rear.

"Has he gone?" asked Lupita.

"Yes," said Pablo. They spoke in Spanish now. "I really think he is going to see Corbett. I told him about Arroyo del Diablo. He might stop there tonight. What happened here after I left?"

"Not much fight in this bunch," said Rodriguez. "With Prescott out cold, no one else wanted to try him. What was his name?"

"Joe Trento."

"Well, everyone could see that he's good with a gun. Nobody wanted to call him out. They took Prescott over to Butler's place. They're all out there now, I think."

The next morning, Lupita rose at dawn, packed some food and slipped from the *jacale* she shared with her elderly father. She galloped across the plain to Arroyo del Diablo where she walked her pony up and down, softly calling Joe's name, but there was no answer. Joe Trento had already gone.

CHAPTER 7

THE COUNTRY WAS broken and hilly now. Far to the east, and not so far to the west, Joe could see hazy brown mountains. The going was rougher, but Joe felt better. He had been insecure out in the open desert; this was more to his liking.

Joe was reminded of the hills and ravines of Texas where he had worked popping longhorns out of the mesquite thickets. Later these animals would be replaced with specially bred white-faced cattle, grazing on flat prairies to the north. But for a time, Joe grew expert at negotiating the wickedly rugged arroyos and thickets, flushing out the wily longhorns who would just as soon charge at you as they would hightail it the other way.

Joe knew that there were particular dangers associated with these badlands. Rattlers, Indians, and outlaws could be lurking. Joe knew how and where to avoid the snakes. As for Indians, he thought he was safe. The Apache were based in more mountainous areas, although a roving band could be found anywhere. Navajo . . . far to the north, along with Pueblo tribes.

The greatest danger was from outlaws. Mexican bandit gangs prowled the area, finding bountiful opportunities for ambush and plunder, then disappearing into the rugged and inaccessible canyons. It was a lucrative business, for any traveler to El Paso, Tucson, Yuma, or almost any other destination inevitably had to pass through the rugged, narrow mountain passes.

Any gang spotting Joe moving alone could swoop down and kill him for his horse and possessions. All Joe could do was avoid high ground where he might be more easily seen. He also kept a cautious eye on the surrounding country and the trail he was following. Hopefully, he could avoid coming upon anyone unexpectedly. If attacked, he stood a reasonable chance of slipping away among the rocks and gullies.

He was glad that Blue had received some attention from Pablo. This type of travel was tough on the gelding; however, the horse also seemed to be more comfortable now that they had left the flatlands behind. The animal, like its rider, had experience in rough country, and in case of trouble, Joe would not hesitate to give the horse its head and let it choose an escape route through the scrub.

He rode late into the day. He felt fairly fresh after his night's sleep in Arroyo del Diablo. When the sun was about an hour from its set, Joe began to scout the surrounding country for water. He would not actually camp close to a watering place, for such would likely be visited by other men and beasts. However, he hoped to find a drink for Blue in order to preserve what was in his canteens for himself.

He had been stopping periodically and climbing a suitable hill or pile of rock. Lying on his belly, he would scan the country below, looking for certain signs. Anything green appearing in the landscape hinted at water, as did unusual animal activity. Joe also searched for game trails, especially those of mule deer, as he rode.

The young man had managed to put his recent trouble in San Martin somewhat out of his mind. The events in Maysville and his worries about reaching Corbett had occupied his thoughts instead. As the day closed, however, and weariness and hunger began to creep back over him, so did his concerns about the Milsteads and his trouble with the law. For all he knew, he may have killed two men while making his escape. He had come very close to killing a man—or being killed—in Maysville.

He had to concentrate on a plan of action for disproving the murder accusation and handling the Milsteads. What, exactly, would he ask Corbett to help him to do?

Joe lay on his belly on top of a rise. He surveyed a flat, open valley below, strewn with rock, but open nevertheless. Good sign and bad sign. Good in that Joe spied several spots displaying unusually green vegetation, which meant there was water. But to get to it he would have to cross the small plain, several miles wide, in order to reach any of the potential watering spots, and to continue on his trail.

The sun was falling rapidly, but Joe figured that darkness would be neither an advantage nor a disadvantage. The bandits that he was concerned about would be almost as vigilant at night as during the day. Early morning might actually be the best time to cross.

But right now Blue needed a drink, so Joe set his sights on the nearest clump of green, about a hundred yards off. At the first sign of trouble they would hightail it back up the hill.

They reached the brush growing at the base of a huge rock. The ground on one side was flattened and worn, and this was where the most vegetation grew. Joe could tell that at times a small stream rushed through this spot. The young stockman parted the bushes and crushed several to the ground under his boot. With the aid of his knife and a flat rock, he dug at the sandy soil. It was damp several inches down. He worked until he had made a depression the size of a large washbasin, squatted down, and waited. Blue nickered softly. The bottom of the depression grew darker and damper, and within a few minutes, several inches of water had filled the hole. He let the horse drink. It wasn't much at all.

The pair waited another ten minutes—a little more this time. Joe let Blue pull at the leaves of the bushes for a while, then drink again. The sun dipped lower behind the hills. Leading the gelding, Joe retraced his trail back out of the valley, down into a nearby ravine, then up into a small canyon he had spotted earlier. The canyon narrowed as it led upward, and at one point there was some buffalo grass that had caught hold, grown, withered, and died. Joe stopped there so that the horse could chew the brown stems. He walked on a ways farther to make sure there was another way out. Soon the arroyo widened and sloped up into more hills.

Joe Trento returned to the grassy spot and made a dry camp. He unsaddled the horse, spread his bedroll on the ground, and sat. He considered trying to shoot some game, but quickly dismissed the idea. It would attract too much attention. It was twilight now anyway. Tomorrow he'd be in Morelos, if all went well. Late afternoon or evening probably, but he'd not starve. He still had money and he'd eat right away—not just a plate of beans, either, but a real meal.

This made Joe think of Lupita, and how pleasant it had been to have her sit with him, if only for a few minutes. He had known girls over the years, but none for very long. He had never stayed in one place. Sometimes the drives would take him back to the same towns again and again, but soon a new rail head would spring up and Joe would follow the steers to a different stockyard in a new town. The cowboys never knew where the next drive would go, so they could tell the girls nothing with certainty.

Nevertheless, sitting with Lupita had reminded him of how fine a woman's company could be.

Joe thought of Elizabeth Milstead. He wondered what her company would be like. Probably very fine. She seemed very intelligent, sophisticated.

Joe lay down and rolled himself in his blankets. He tried to focus on the details of the murder accusation, looking for a way to prove that the Milsteads were lying. Instead, his mind kept wandering back to Elizabeth. He wondered what kind of life she led up at the Milstead place. What kind of future was in store for a girl like her, or Millie— or any of the ranch women whose lives were led in rugged isolation?

He knew that some girls left when they were old enough, and moved back east or to a large city. But some were fond of the ranch life and the wilderness and desired to make their homes there.

"What do you think, Blue? Would a girl like that want to live in an old lean-to with me?" The horse pricked up his ears for a moment, then went back to munching grass.

After a few months of being prodded roughly awake in the morning, a young drover learned to get up and into his boots at the first sleepy chirps of the daybirds. So Joe was used to rising early. The next morning, he was up before the sun and moving almost immediately.

He wished to be across the small valley and into cover again before any desperadoes might wake up and start looking around. Joe led Blue out to the hole he had dug, which again held several inches of water. The horse drank. Joe stepped into the saddle and they moved out.

The cowboy nudged Blue into a trot, figuring to take advantage of the flatness. The low, rising sun shone from one end of the valley and suddenly reflected off something.

Instantly, Blue was at a run, flat out, Joe's face plastered to the horse's neck. Whether the animal had also seen the glint and anticipated Joe's spurs, the man was not sure, but their sudden move foiled the gunman's aim and a bullet sped silently behind them.

Another shot crashed through the brush and chipped the stones ahead of them. Trento reined the horse to the right without breaking its stride, then back left again. They continued this zigzag course and reached the rocky slope on the opposite side. The gelding lunged up the hillside, its hooves slipping and popping on the loose stones. Joe reined up behind a small outcropping and dismounted. Crawling quickly to the edge, he looked across the expanse to the heap of rocks from which the shots had originated.

There they were, three of them, mounted now, their ponies stepping and sliding down to the valley floor. They were galloping across the flat space toward Joe's new hideout.

Joe reached up and pulled the Winchester from the saddle boot, shouldered, aimed, and levered off a pair of shots. The outlaws sat up in the saddle, looked surprised, but continued their gallop. They were several hundred yards off. Joe fired again, this time hitting one of them, who clutched his side. The three ponies slid to an abrupt halt.

The cutthroats were slowly realizing their predicament. The three of them had rushed out into an open space where they made very fine targets, while their intended victim was hidden safely up above. They would be cut to pieces before they even got close.

Joe whistled a low one over their heads. It convinced the trio to whirl around and lash their mounts back to the other side, leaving a cloud of dust in their wake.

Joe chuckled. "I'll bet those boys didn't expect much of a fight, Blue. They didn't seem to be expecting us."

Joe racked the rifle twice more and sent a few shots across the valley. Then, still grinning, he crawled to the winded gelding. He led the horse further into the rocks before mounting.

Despite the relative early morning cool, the big horse was sweating from the run and was still a bit winded. Joe promised himself that he'd start taking better care of the gelding soon. Normally, a short sprint like that would no more tucker out the big animal than climbing a flight of stairs would wind a young coon dog. Blue was part "blooded" horse, the result of crossing English stallions on local western mares, a popular method of combining the size and stamina of the thoroughbred with the quickness and cow sense of the western pony. A horse like Blue could spend the entire day dashing back and forth among a bunch of longhorns and not breathe as hard as he had just now. After almost five days of poor food and water and little rest, the horse was weakening, Joe feared.

Horse and rider again found the scant trail leading southward and continued to wind their way through the riotous array of rocks, brush, and stunted mesquite. Joe felt sure that the outlaws would not risk being picked off while crossing the basin. They would have to circle around, keeping to the higher hills and arroyos, then find Joe's trail on the southern side. Joe knew how to make good time through such country, so he expected no further trouble. Still, as the morning wore on, he dismounted frequently in order to peruse his backtrail from some vantage point.

CHAPTER 8

JOE TRENTO LOOKED over the busy saloon with mixed feelings. He'd drunk his fill in dozens of watering holes throughout the cattle country to the north and east. Many of the towns had large, busy "devil's additions" for drinking and whoring some ways from the more respectable business districts. Dodge, Wichita—Joe was familiar with them all. So here in Morelos, sitting at a fancy bar in a crowded saloon, he felt almost at home. But at the same time, somehow, he felt uneasy.

For one thing, his dress and general condition made him stand out. The place had its share of hard cases, both Mexican and Anglo, cowboys and card sharps, drunkards and plain regular folk. But Joe was a sight to stare at—his face crusty, bruised, sunburned, and mustachioed; wearing beat-up clothes and boots, and Pablo's sombrero over long dirty hair. More than one newcomer, upon entering the saloon, avoided the bar stools immediately next to Joe. Joe knew he was attracting attention and that was the last thing he wanted.

In addition, the atmosphere and flavor of Morelos were different from the western towns to which Joe was accustomed. This was a border town, a stone's throw from Mexico. It had a foreignness about it; an unknown quality. This wasn't a cattle town, full of drovers passing through and looking for some fun.

It was not a large town—perhaps less than a thousand people, Joe figured, but it had an energy about it. Lots of coming and going. He could see why Lupita was impressed with the place.

"*¿Uno mas, amigo?*" The Mexican bartender approached. "Another beer for you?"

"Sure, why not?" Joe slid his glass across. He had pushed hard all day, and had made good time, arriving just after supper. He was sure that he'd left his attackers far behind, if they had continued to follow him.

He had counted his coins and paper money before arriving in town. There was enough to put Blue somplace decent for a few days, buy a few good meals, a few beers, and get a room for at least one night. He'd already found a stable and left horse and gear there, except for the Winchester. For some reason, he'd felt inclined to carry it even though he still had Parker's six-gun.

He ordered another beer and relaxed, looking around and listening. Next, he would find a meal. His stomach ached with hunger. The liveryman had mentioned a hotel and restaurant down the street.

The barkeep brought the glass. Joe needed to establish that Thad was actually in Morelos. He couldn't risk exhausting his funds here in town only to find out later that his friend was not here.

"*Amigo,*" Joe called to the bartender. "I'm looking for an old friend of mine. Name of Thaddeus Corbett. Know him?"

The Mexican had previously cast curious glances at Joe. Now he studied the young cowboy's poor condition, took in the six-gun, worn leather, the beaten and tired face.

"I know many men in Morelos. Everyone comes here to drink and play cards. Corbett? There are many gringo names . . . I don't pay attention."

"This man is quick with a gun."

"There are many like that here. I do not know anything about them." His eyes were on the revolver strapped to Joe's thigh.

I should've expected that, thought Joe. He thinks I'm a troublemaker, someone gunning for Thad, and he doesn't want to get in the middle. Maybe Thad has had trouble here already. . . .

The barkeep turned away.

Joe realized that he would have to change his tactics. Anyone he asked directly would likely react the same as the bartender. Where else would information be available? Perhaps from the marshal. He pondered this. There was a chance that word had been telegraphed by Billy Heywood, or even by the Milsteads, about an escaped prisoner. Regardless, a lawman would tend to be suspicious of Joe in his present state, and the dusty cowboy had no convincing story to tell.

If he knew in what occupation Corbett was currently employed, he might find him by pretending to seek out his services. Was he working as a cowhand? A laborer? A craftsman in town? Joe decided that Thad wouldn't be involved in any common occupation. His friend had made his living as a hired gun for the most part. Well, that was a thought.

"Mister? Couldn't help overhearin'." Joe looked up to see a gray-eyed, shaggy-haired cowboy. The man looked just about as dusty and worn-out as Joe. "You asked about Corbett." The man shuffled his feet. Seemed a little nervous.

"That's right," said Joe. "You know him?"

"Well, I've met 'im once, and I'm here to say that Corbett's got quite a few friends around these parts, including me. I suspect you've got some kind of business with him, and prob'ly none too friendly neither. Well, Corbett's tryin' to avoid trouble around town and doin' a good job of it, too, so I advise you just forget about lookin' for 'im and cut out."

Good lord, Joe thought, Thad ought to run for office, as popular as he seemed to be lately. Joe decided to play his hand.

"You can go to hell, mister! I don't take advice from the

likes of you." Joe talked plenty loud. "Thad Corbett is a liar and a thief. I'll find him if I have to hang around this dump for a year!" It was a long shot, but it seemed like the only way.

The gray-eyed wrangler turned red in the face. Joe turned back to his beer. The wrangler began to speak, stopped, then simply said, "Well, I'm warnin' you!" He turned and stalked off.

Joe heard a sudden buzz of conversation coming from several tables. He kept his back to the room and hoped he'd made the right move. If word got to Thad that a tough-looking gun was bad-mouthing him around town, he'd eventually have to come for a look-see. Joe only hoped that one of Corbett's self-appointed protectors didn't get in the way first.

He finished his beer and left. He felt a dozen eyes on his back as he walked out. Several patrons stared openly at him, some with curiosity in their eyes, others with plain hatred.

Outside, he felt like he truly was in old Mexico, even though technically he was not. The town looked like a Mexican village. Joe walked down the stone walk toward the restaurant. He must have looked like one of the *ladrones* from the hills, with big sombrero, guns, scraping spurs. People got out of his way as he came.

The restaurant, like most of the town, was of adobe and brick construction. However, a second story had been added that was wooden. Attached to the back of the edifice was another frame extension of two stories. It all made for a peculiar-looking, but somehow appealing combination. No doubt some gringo's attempt to Americanize the hotel.

Joe Trento entered and seated himself. He ordered a meal of steak and potatoes. While waiting, he thought about what had just transpired in the saloon. Surely his words with the bartender and the wrangler would cause an explosion of rumors and gossip around town. Thad

Corbett would not come gunning right off, since he was trying to avoid just such trouble. However, he might come around surreptitiously to sneak a look. That would be best. Corbett would recognize Joe—it had been only a year since their last meeting—and the search would be over. Meantime, Joe must be careful not to be too boisterous. Some other local tough might find an urge to call him out.

After eating, Joe decided to head back to the livery. Even though he had a gut feeling that he'd find his old friend soon, he wanted to take no chances. The few dollars he had left would become very important if he didn't find Corbett and had to head out on his own. The question was, even though Corbett was skilled at handling the kind of trouble Joe was having, would he be willing to get involved? Could the two of them do it alone?

The important thing was that he had escaped his pursuers and contacted some formidable help. Well, almost. Joe was certain that Corbett would have plenty of ideas about how to get out of this mess back in San Martin. After all, folks hired him, paid him good money, just to handle this kind of trouble.

He walked along feeling pretty good about things. At least his spirits were much improved over the past few nights. Perhaps it was the food and drink, or maybe the atmosphere of a lively town. Maybe it was the sense of accomplishment he now had regarding his progress toward finding the old gunfighter.

At any rate, with his mind more at ease and a good meal in his belly, Joe was looking forward to a soft bed, even if it was just a bale of straw.

The evening was quieting down rapidly . . . no Kansas trail town here. Folks were mostly home in bed at this hour, although several saloons and the hotel all had some patrons keeping the lanterns burning.

A boy sleeping on a cot woke up when Joe entered the

barn. Joe was rummaging around in his gear, untying his bedroll.

"You need something, mister? You fixing to leave tonight?"

"No, sir!" said Joe. "I'm not moving from this spot till morning, 'cept to piss, maybe." He flipped the boy a coin through the moonlight. "You don't mind if I bunk down next to old Blue, here, do you? I've already got my own feed and water."

"I guess it's all right. You've already paid for your horse . . . guess it's all right." The boy, half asleep, was too tired to argue. He returned to bed.

Joe threw his blankets down on some clean straw in the stall next to Blue's. He sat and pulled his boots off. Tomorrow could be the day, he thought. If he found Thad tomorrow, he'd go to the hotel and get himself a bath, by God. Or maybe Corbett would have a place.

Joe began to doze and was asleep before his thoughts could turn to the Milsteads, or San Martin, or Lupita and Elizabeth.

There was a well out in the yard behind the livery, and Joe cleaned himself up as best he could. It was a bright, pretty morning, and he felt fresh and rested. He donned a fresh shirt, his revolver, the sombrero, and walked back into town.

The thing to do, he figured, was to have a cup of coffee at the restaurant, then mosey through some of the establishments in town. If Thad Corbett came out, Joe wanted to be visible.

It wouldn't be hard. People still stared at his rough-looking clothes and haggard face. Joe hadn't looked in a mirror for a while, but he knew that events of the past few days must have left some beautiful bruises on his face . . . at least judging by the way it felt and the way folks stared.

Joe entered the restaurant and sat. A few glances, a

stare. Nothing too unusual. He ordered coffee and savored it. The place was clean and well kept. Whoever was responsible for planning and outfitting the place was obviously trying for a touch of elegance out here on the frontier.

Walking out, Joe almost ran into the marshal. Each mumbled an apology and headed off in different directions. Damn, thought Joe. The last person he needed attention from was the law! If his tough talk in the saloon the previous night had spread all over town as he'd intended, then the marshal had no doubt heard about it. Any constable worth his salt was always on the lookout for trouble. If the lawman felt that gunplay or a fight was forthcoming, he just might decide to head it off. That would mean getting rid of Joe, most likely. After his experience in San Martin, he was determined to spend no more time behind bars.

The marshal had given Joe a surprised look, nothing more. But something told Joe Trento that the lawman knew he was the desperado folks were talking about.

Joe walked briskly without looking back. He wanted to get out of sight in case the man decided to come have a talk. He ducked into the general store.

He had better buy something so as not to irritate the merchant. No one liked a mean-looking *pistolero* hanging around, making the ladies nervous. Joe looked at some sweets in jars, then bought some jerky from the owner, who smiled at him. Didn't seem too upset. Joe relaxed a little. He browsed for a few more minutes and then left.

He decided to head back to the livery, take a look at Blue, maybe give him a good brushing himself. If Thad came looking, someone would probably suggest the livery. Later, Joe would visit a saloon or two.

The gelding nickered a greeting upon seeing Joe. Poor old boy, thought Joe, probably can't figure out what all this night riding and strange towns is about. He checked the horse over. Seemed to be in fair condition. He carefully lifted and examined each hoof. Not bad. He picked out some stones.

Joe groomed Blue for a while, then walked to the front of the barn. The boy was sitting outside on a bench, rubbing an old saddle.

"Mornin'," said Joe.

"Mornin', mister."

"Nice sunny day today."

"Every day is sunny in Morelos. Hardly ever rains." The boy barely glanced up from his work.

"That so?" said Joe. He leaned in the doorway, chewing on a straw, and looked out at the street.

"Reckon you'll sleep in the stall again tonight? My pa . . . he don't like it."

"You told your pa?"

"Well, yes." The boy looked up, embarrassed. "But he'd a known anyway. Folks have been talkin' about you. Some saw you head up here last night and they told my pa."

"Well, you tell your pa I won't stay any longer than I have to. Maybe not even tonight. I'll pay him extra though, if he wants it."

"I don't know . . ." The youngster was eyeballing Joe's big gun. The dead marshal's gun, actually. "You lookin' to shoot Corbett? That's what everyone says."

Joe was a little surprised. The word had certainly gotten around. "Believe it or not, son," Joe said, confiding in the boy, "I'm not lookin' to shoot anyone. Thad Corbett is an old friend of mine. I've come to get his help with some trouble I'm having up on my spread. Problem is, no one will tell me where he's at."

"You don't look like you need a hired gun," said the boy. "You look like a hired gun yourself." The boy's face reddened, but he continued. "And you don't look like no rancher neither." The boy reddened more.

Joe smiled. "Well, I won't be if I don't find Corbett. Back when we were driving cattle up to Kansas—"

"Hey! You're Joe Trento!" blurted the boy.

CHAPTER 9

JOE WAS STUNNED. It felt strange to hear his name spoken so unexpectedly. "That's right! How'd you know?"

"I've heard Corbett talk about you. He's been down here lots of times to see my pa."

"Do you know where he stays?"

"Sure. Right outside of town. South. He's got a ranch. Well, not a ranch really. He's got a cabin back there in the hills and a bunch of brood mares."

"I'll be damned," said Joe Trento.

"I've heard him tell my pa about a cowboy he used to ride with who has a place up north. Named Joe Trento. That must be you."

"Reckon so," said Joe. He started to get his things together, planning to head out pronto. "Much obliged, son. You've saved me a great deal of time and trouble."

"Don't mention it. He may not be there, though. Sometimes he up and leaves all of a sudden. Stays away for weeks sometimes."

Joe saddled up and got his gear together. Old Blue felt frisky after the rest and the grooming, and tossed his head playfully as they trotted down the street.

Joe was glad he had trusted his instinct to be honest with the boy. But he should have questioned the boy yesterday. The livery was the first place he had visited, and a stable boy would be a likely person to know someone like Corbett. Joe had wasted time and taken a big chance putting on the hard-case act.

He was riding through downtown Morelos, heading south. The boy had described a turnoff Joe should take about four miles outside of town. He had just passed the saloon from the night before and was approaching the restaurant when he heard a sudden scuffle of feet, the bang of swinging doors. He looked back and saw that two men had rushed out of the saloon and jumped onto horses. They wheeled about and galloped off to the north, then cut down an alley. A third man burst through the doors and trotted across the street, glancing briefly up at Joe.

Joe resumed his jog southward, wondering what was going on. Seconds later, as he was passing the hotel, he heard approaching hoofbeats. Suddenly, the two cowboys slid to a stop in front of him, blocking his way. They had apparently galloped through the back alleys in order to cut him off.

Damn, thought Joe. Trouble. "What's the problem, boys?"

"You're headin' the wrong way, mister," said one. "You want to be headin' back north."

"Now wait a minute, fellers, I know what direction I'm headin', and—"

The man on the left decided not to hear Joe out. He began to draw. A shot erupted from Joe's gun and the slug hit the other man's .45, knocking it to the ground.

Joe's two obstacles were stunned. All three men sat their horses for a moment, Joe's pistol covering the other two.

"Now listen here—" Joe began.

"Hold it, son!" A voice from behind him. Joe looked over his shoulder. It was the marshal, pointing a shotgun at his back! "Off the horse, young feller. Let's move!"

"Marshal, I just want to leave town!"

"And I want you to climb off that horse. Now!"

Joe stepped down. "Marshal, I—"

"Drop that gun and head up to the jailhouse!"

"But—"

"Enough! Get moving or I'll unload some lead on your boots!"

Joe moved. The jailhouse was several buildings down, across from the saloon. Joe entered, followed by the marshal.

Inside, the man who had run from the saloon was half leaning, half sitting on the marshal's desk, smiling smugly.

"You can go, Avery, and thanks," said the marshal. Avery ambled out the door. "Sit there," the lawman said to Joe. He indicated a wooden chair. Joe sat with a sigh. The marshal sat across from him, still pointing the scatter gun.

Smart man, thought Joe. He hadn't walked out into the street with just a revolver riding in a holster. He'd grabbed a long gun and had had it up and pointing, in control of the situation before Joe even knew he was there.

"Now, Mister Quick-With-a-Gun," the marshal began, "we've got ourselves a problem. Seems like you're determined to make some trouble here for one of our more popular citizens." Joe sighed, shook his head. "I don't want to hear your sad story," the lawman added quickly. "I've heard them all. I don't care much for the likes of Corbett myself, but so far he's kept his nose clean in Morelos. He's not wanted anywhere, he's employed, he doesn't come to town much, and he's got friends . . . kind of a hero around here. What else he does or has done, I don't care."

"Marshal, Thad Corbett is an old friend of mine." Joe finally got a word in. "I've known him for years. I made like I was after him because no one would tell me where he stays."

The marshal raised an eyebrow and appeared amused. "Young feller, I don't know who you are or where you're from, but I've the sincere feeling that if you spent the rest of the day here in my jail, I'd sure be able to find something out."

Probably so, thought Joe wearily.

"Fact is," the marshal continued, "I don't have enough

to hold you, except for maybe the threats you made last night."

The marshal sat back, thinking a moment. "I'd run you out of town, headin' north, except you'd just find your way back around, most likely—"

"The boy!" exclaimed Joe. "The boy at the livery knows! He'd heard Corbett talk to his pa about me!"

The marshal seemed unimpressed. "In you go, son. I don't like the smell of this whole business. I'm going to do some checking." He rose to usher Joe into the cell. Joe started to protest again.

"Lock him up good, Marshal," said a voice. "This slippery snake is wanted in every trail town in Kansas . . . by a few dozen bar girls, that is!"

Joe's head snapped around. There stood Thaddeus Corbett, hands on his hips, wearing a wide grin.

"Corbett!" Joe exclaimed, jumping up. "Damn you!" Thad Corbett threw his head back and laughed loudly. The marshal sat, dumbfounded.

"Had to ride in and see what all the talk was about," said Corbett. "I've had a parade of folks out to my place telling of a mean-looking killer in town after my hide."

"I figured you'd get the message," Joe said. "Too many tight-lipped citizens in this town for a man to come calling the regular way."

"Uh . . . just a minute," said the marshal. He looked at Corbett. "You know him?"

"Marshal, I happen to be like a god to this boy. He follows me wherever I go in order to admire me."

"Well, you already know he's been in every saloon in town threatening to shoot you on sight."

"Only one saloon, Marshal," said Joe. "And like I told you, I only said those things to flush him out. Looks like it worked."

"Awfully strange way of going about it," mumbled the lawman.

"The boy's been a bit touched ever since I've known him," said Corbett. "Sorry if he's raised a ruckus."

"You sure he ain't on the run?"

"Marshal," said Joe, "I've had trouble with some men up north where I've got a spread. I've got a partner still up there, and I've had to ride straight through to get some help. That's the truth." It was not the entire truth certainly, but basically it was true.

Corbett spoke up, his tone serious now. "Joe here has had his share of scrapes with the law, but so far as I know, he's always steered clear of serious trouble. He ought to be pretty clean."

"Well, I guess I've wasted enough of my time with you," said the marshal. "Corbett, if he's a friend of yours, get him out of here. And let's have no more foolishness like last night in the saloon. Someone could have gotten hurt."

Corbett winked at Joe. "Don't worry, Marshal, I'll keep him out of trouble."

Outside, Corbett whacked Joe on the back and laughed loudly again. Joe grinned and glanced, amused, at several groups of onlookers across the street. The folks were staring and talking bewilderedly to one another.

"Joey, you sure never do anything average. You always have a fancy way of going about a job, don't you?" The two leaned on the hitching post and looked at the street.

"I didn't have time to go any other road," Joe said. "Folks around here all act like you're kin. I'd have had better luck askin' that bartender to take his daughter back to the livery for the night. Same up in Maysville, only at least they told me something—"

"Pablo Orazco! I bet you ran into Pablo in that little cantina."

"Yep. He even gave me his hat."

"Haven't been through Maysville now for a good spell. How'd you run across him?"

"Well, there's only the one cantina in town, and as I was saying, I mentioned your name, just to see, you know, and Lupita said she knew you. And she introduced me to Pablo."

Thad smiled and was quiet for a moment. "I'll tell you Joey, this part of the country is a heap different from Kansas. Why, back there, a man knew nothing but the trail . . . for years sometimes. There were the towns and the saloons, and the stores and hotels, but that was part of the trail too. All that's a young man's world. Guns and cards and such.

"Now, when I quit trailing beeves to earn my supper, I found out there are a lot of other people besides cowboys and bar girls out here. Prob'ly back in Kansas too—we just didn't see 'em. Most of these other folks are here to settle— white and Mexican—and they're not all of them packing guns like we're used to. Trouble is, plenty of the old boys from Texas figure the whole country is Dodge City. You know, poker and ladies and whiskey. Not all of them are out to make an honest living, either."

Joe wondered what Corbett was driving at.

"The honest folks, they're looking to settle nice, quiet towns, safe countryside, like back East. We've got some law out here, but it's mighty weak in most places. I can't say I've never broken a law or hurt another man, but all in all, I've never gone out of my way to give people trouble, especially innocent folk.

"A couple times now, I've been near a situation where some hard cases were bustin' up a place or roughin' up a fellow, like up in Maysville, and I've stepped in. I can still clear leather faster than most men I'm likely to come up against. Seems when these folks see a fast gun bein' used for good instead of bad, they get stirred up. They like it."

Corbett paused a moment and looked at Joe. He chuckled, embarrassed at being so serious. "I guess the way I look at it, there's as much good to be done with a six-gun as bad. I've had to turn down certain jobs and seek out others, like this one comin' up, but it has paid off. Instead of bein' run off by the local lawman, I'm welcome here. I can stay permanent if I want."

"What's the job comin' up?" asked Joe.

Corbett stood and slapped his hands on his dusty trousers. "We've talked enough about this old man," he said. "What I want to know is, what the hell are you doing in Morelos, and why do you look like a wore-out hound dog?"

"Broke out of jail," said Joe, primarily to enjoy the shocked look on Corbett's face.

"What?"

"Come on," said Joe, "I've been promising myself a bath and some grub. How about settin' for a spell and I'll tell you a story."

"You're on," said Corbett. "I've got an old horse trough out at my place that you can use, but I could use a decent dinner myself."

Joe told his story over plates of roast venison and beans, washed down with hot coffee. Thad Corbett ate and listened while Joe talked between mouthfuls.

"So that's about it," concluded Joe. "If I ride back into San Martin, the deputy would have to jail me again and tell the judge the facts, which means in jail I'd stay, since the judge most likely won't believe my story. If the Milsteads spot me first, it'll be a shoot-out. If they even hear that I'm in jail again, they'll raise hell, just like last time. I need some time to get back to the ranch and talk to Al. I need a plan . . . and I'll need some help."

Corbett was quiet for a long time. Finally he swallowed his last bite of meat and spoke. "You're in a fix, all right. Way I see it, you'll be hard-pressed to find actual proof you didn't kill the man. On the other hand, the only evidence they have is the girl. And now that her brothers have killed the marshal, who knows where they've gone and where the girl is? You say she seemed scared, sort of disinclined to talk about it?"

"Sure did. Her cousin too. Elizabeth. Appeared like she knew the whole thing was a lie. I figure the girl probably saw something that night, most likely one of her own kin doing the killing. Maybe she couldn't see who it was in the dark, and her pa pushed her into claiming it was me."

"I think the main thing is to get you back on your spread," said Corbett. "I've been tangled up in my share of range wars and such around these parts. It's not always a matter of which side of the law you're on, especially outside of town. What pulls more weight is appearances. You, bein' way down here, on the run, like . . . that won't look good to nobody, law or otherwise.

"Now, seein' as how one of these boys has killed a lawman, they're in the same fix as you. Were an outside lawman to come in and find each of you on your property, lookin' down gun barrels at each other, them havin' killed a marshal, you maybe killed a hired hand . . . what would a feller think? Seems like a peace officer would go after the other bunch first."

"You saying I should just ride on back to my place, take on the deputy and the Milstead clan?"

"I'm bettin' the deputy has got his hands full in town. I don't think he'll ride out and try to bring you in, not right off, so long as you mind your own business. 'Course, you'll need more guns than just you and Al—to handle the Milsteads, that is."

"That's why I came, old buddy. I knew that alone I didn't stand a chance. You mentioned a job coming up. Does that mean you can't—"

"Tell you what, Joey," said Corbett, "another few days won't matter much. May even help. Get those Milsteads to let down their guard some. You were right . . . if you had

stayed up there and tried to hold the fort with Al, they'd
have prob'ly killed you both before they sobered up.

"For right now, there's a Citizen's Committee here in
Morelos that's hired me to do a job, and I need good men.
You throw in with me for a few days, then we'll head up
north together. What do you say?"

"What kind of job?" Joe was a little suspicious, and quite
a bit disappointed.

"This part of the country is growing like wildfire,"
explained Corbett. "Morelos, since it's been a Mexican
settlement for years, naturally has a head start as a trading
post. Lots of outfitters heading north and west start out
from here. Lots of folks heading back east stop through
here. Quite a bit of business to be done, Joe, and most
folks like it that way. You've not been in town long, but
maybe even you've heard of how bad the hills around here
are. I mean Mexican gangs. It's rough land—plenty of
hideouts. Plenty of travelers loaded with gear and grub.
The *banditos* can take their pick of dozens of ambushes in
and out of Morelos, and believe me, they do."

"I believe you," said Joe, "and I'll wager I know where
one of their places is."

CHAPTER 10

THAD CORBETT RAISED his eyebrows, and Joe related his experience of crossing the basin and being shot at and chased.

Corbett thought for a moment. "Not a lot of folks come in on that trail, but it wouldn't surprise me if Deligro had a few scouts posted out there . . . just to watch for a few days and report back."

"Deligro?"

"He's the *jefe* around here. At least of the gang controlling this part of the territory. Sometimes they roam, but mostly they do their work right around here. Some of 'em even come to town quite a bit. A few may live here—who knows? The Mexicans say there are over fifty of 'em."

"And you want to go after fifty outlaws with four or five men?" Joe asked, a little perturbed.

"Not exactly. First of all, there are at least two men from town, the liveryman and a saloon owner—pretty good men—who stand to lose a lot if travelers are scared away from Morelos. Also, there are two ranchers from outside of town who lose a lot of beef to the gang, and they'll each bring along hired hands. I figure we'll have a dozen men."

"Still not much of an army," said Joe. He was irritated by the irony that he had come to Morelos to enlist Corbett's help and now his friend was turning the tables on him— Corbett was recruiting him.

"Look, Joey," said Thad Corbett, leaning forward, "you don't think fifty killer Mexicans are going to come galloping down a hillside, do you? Maybe there are fifty in the gang—I don't know—but they don't all travel in a pack.

Deligro's got them in three or four groups, maybe more, scattered around the hills—like the ones that took after you. It doesn't take that many outlaws to rob a wagonload of homesteaders. This way, he covers more area . . . attracts less attention."

"What's your plan?" Joe asked.

"Take a freight wagon, hide some of the men in it, and head west. Two of us will head out, separate, and shadow the wagon, about half a mile off. It'll be rough going, but I don't think the gang will take notice of two men out in the hills. They'll be interested in watching the road. When the time comes, those two can ride in and open up on the gang's flank."

"How'll they know the time?"

"They'll hear shooting if nothing else. More'n likely, they'll find places to stop and look down on the road now and then, see what's going on. Listen, Joe, all the others are in this as volunteers. I'm getting paid to head up the whole thing. You throw in and I'll cut you in for fifty dollars. It'll help make up for the time and money you're losing coming all the way down here."

That it would, thought Joe. What choice did he have, anyway? He couldn't leave without Corbett. He needed his mind and muscle for the task waiting in San Martin. And Corbett was obviously obligated to carry out the plans he'd made with the townspeople.

And he probably honestly needed Joe's help with the job—who could tell what kind of fighters the others would turn out to be? Joe couldn't sit in town for three or four days while Corbett was out hunting outlaws.

"What d'ya say, Joey? It'll be like old times, riding together. All we need to do is convince Deligro to pack up and find new territory. After that, we'll head north . . . only a few days."

"Okay," said Joe, "I'm in."

★ ★ ★

The next morning Carter Andersen's horse grunted with relief as the fat man swung out of the saddle and hit the ground. His two men also stepped down and followed their boss between the cholla bushes and on up to Corbett's cabin.

Joe Trento stood outside, watching the men. He was feeling pretty good: he'd had several good meals in a row now, as well as a good night's sleep.

They would spend the morning finalizing their plans and preparing the wagon, which would then be brought to the livery in town. Once there, Blake Sutter, the livery-man, and Van Brooks, the owner of the Gold Mine saloon, would make a show of outfitting the freighter for a long trip, greasing axles, hitching up horses, testing harness. This might attract the attention of one of Deligro's scouts or it might not. But if it did, the outlaws would then watch for the wagon's departure the following morning and alert the rest of the gang. The wagon would disappear into the barn that evening and reappear in the early morning hours, looking loaded down and ready for a trip.

Thad Corbett appeared in the doorway of his cabin just as Andersen was about to say howdy to Joe. He spoke to Corbett instead.

"Mornin'," Corbett replied. "Obliged to you gentlemen for ridin' in here this mornin'. I think we'll wrap this up in an hour or so and you can all get back to ranching. Until tomorrow, that is."

"Sounds fine," said Andersen. "I'm itching to hear how you plan to cut down this Deligro rascal. These here are two of my men, Colin McCray and Hank Dowell."

Corbett nodded. "This here is Joe Trento, an old partner of mine." Joe stood up and nodded to the men. Hoofbeats popped down in the road, and the group turned to watch another man trot up the trail to Corbett's cabin. "That's Wade Scandal," said Corbett. Wade Scandal left his horse with the others and approached the group on foot.

"Wade, glad you could come," said Corbett. "You know everyone here except Joe Trento."

"Corbett," said Wade Scandal, "let's get on with it. Most of us here have regular jobs to tend to. You may not, but do us a favor and skip the pleasantries. We'll be doing the real job tomorrow. I don't like taking time away from work to stand around and jaw."

Thad stared at Scandal with steely eyes. Joe had seen that look before. Scandal obviously had no liking for the gunslinger, but if he were Scandal, Joe thought, he wouldn't push Thad Corbett too far.

"Scandal, I know you're all busy men," Corbett's voice was surprisingly friendly, "but I've been hired to head up this job because I've had some experience at it. You men are going to be in some danger tomorrow. I've seen plenty of good men killed, mostly due to carelessness. Spending an hour or two this morning is well worth it, in my opinion, if it will help keep the bunch of us alive. Deligro and his gang are killers, not a gang of schoolboys."

Scandal was quiet. He whacked his worn hat back and forth across his thigh and stared at the resulting dust in the air.

"The wagon's out back," said Corbett. He led the way around the cabin. The group walked over to a large wagon and began looking it over.

Joe leaned his forearms on one of the rear wheels and looked out at the country. The land in back of Corbett's place was a rock-strewn canyon, sloping up and out of sight. In addition to several horses in a nearby corral, Joe spied a dozen more head grazing about a hundred yards out. Thad must have the canyon boxed in at the top, if it wasn't naturally so, thought Joe. Not a fancy operation, but a decent setup, nevertheless. With the possible exception of Wade Scandal, most folks probably felt that Corbett's horse-breaking occupation was a legitimate one. It allowed the citizens of Morelos to more easily accept the *pistolero* as a working man like themselves, even if he was at times a hired gun.

And the work was certainly appropriate. Like all cowboys, during his trail-driving days Corbett used a string of horses out of the remuda. Many were young and half-wild, having run free on the range for months, even years. Each cowboy quickly became skilled at riding the buck out of a new mount each day. Thad would have an advantage over the average bronc-buster; he could turn out well-schooled ranch stock more quickly than most men. This was not as lush and green as the mountainous land that Joe owned, but over time, Corbett would build this place into a nice little spread.

"Blake and Van will load some sacks and canvas and such in here," Corbett was saying, "and fix it so five of us can hunker down inside. When we're attacked, those five can shoot from behind the sacks, or whatever Blake comes up with."

"What'll the rest of us do?" asked Anderson.

"Carter, I'd like you and Van Brooks to drive. You're too big to hide in the back, and I think you'd be best off driving. I want Van up there because he's a businessman in town and it makes sense that he'd be hauling freight somewhere. The last three of us will be riding flank. I want that to be me, Joe, and José Valero—you know Valero, he works out at Wade's place. That leaves the four hired men in the wagon, along with Sutter and you, Scandal. All right?"

"Guess so," said Wade Scandal. "Couldn't spare my men from the ranch today, but they'll be in tonight."

"Well, be sure you fill them in," said Corbett.

"Don't worry, that I will."

"I've met that Valero a time or two," said Andersen, "and I know he's a fine rifle shot. He'll be a good one to have up in the rocks, pecking away at Deligro's bunch."

Corbett nodded, then went on to explain the rest of the

plan. He gave each man detailed instructions. "Aim each shot to kill," he concluded. "Take your time. Don't go blasting off half a dozen shots and not hit anything. We ought to be able to get quite a few of them and run the rest off. Now, there's a chance that we don't drive them off or that the wagon gets pinned down. If they get to moving in on us, then we'll run."

"If there's a chance of that," cut in Scandal, "then maybe this ain't such a great plan."

"I wouldn't risk my neck, or anyone else's, if I didn't think the plan would work," said Corbett. "We'll have them in a cross fire and take them by surprise in the flank—I expect they'll spook and run right off. On the other hand, it doesn't cost us anything to plan a way out if things don't go our way. Blake Sutter has two good horses he says will keep steady and can turn the wagon around almost any-place on that road. Carter will try and do that as soon as the shooting starts, so you'll be headed back toward More-los. If you all decide that the Mexicans are getting too hot, run for town. There'll still be three of us up above, remember, and we'll cover your back end. Any questions?"

Andersen's men went off to catch two of Corbett's horses in order to haul the wagon to town. The rest of the men returned to the front of the building. Wade Scandal mounted up immediately and hurried off to his ranch. Carter Andersen chatted amiably for a few minutes, then rode off as well.

Thad Corbett and Joe Trento went inside to gather their things themselves.

"You reckon things'll go as smoothly as you let on out there," asked Joe, "I mean, be over in a few minutes and all?"

"I do," answered the older man. "Joe, I know I've sort of roped you into this thing. If you feel that you ought to pull out and wait here until it's over, I'll understand."

"No, I said I'm in, and I'm in."

"Well, if I were you, with what you've been through—
the law on your tail, and your own ranch and your partner
maybe in trouble a hundred miles off—well, I'd be reluctant to go out and get myself shot up and maybe unable to
travel. I've been studying on it, and maybe I shouldn't have
pushed you into this thing."

Joe looked out through a small window and watched the
freight wagon, driven by McCray and Dowell, bouncing
down the trail toward the main road.

"Pushed? Hell! I wouldn't miss it for all the gold in
Mexico!" Joe turned and grinned. "Ever since you told me
the plan I've been itching to see if an old man like you can
really still ride and shoot. I'll be there to cover you if you
can't!"

The next morning Joe squatted outside the door of the
livery, partially hidden in the shadows. His ability to sit on
his heels for long periods of time had been acquired
during years of squatting around campfires, often at this
same hour of the day. The skill had served him well on
many occasions.

The town was still asleep. Joe felt sure that all of the
men had arrived unnoticed. Colin McCray and Hank
Dowell had delivered the wagon yesterday afternoon. That
shouldn't have attracted attention—two hired hands returning a wagon. The rest of the men had drifted in
during the night and were now holed up in the livery,
sleeping, with the exception of the stable's owner, Blake
Sutter, who was just now arriving. He was accompanied by
his boy who had spent the previous night at home.

The boy seemed pleased to see Joe hunkered down in
the shadows. He whispered something excitedly to his
father as they passed. Joe stood up and followed the two
inside.

They would have to move quickly now, loading the
wagon, hiding the men, and pulling out. Joe, Corbett, and

José Valero would leave first. The livery was on the northern edge of town, so the three could slide away unnoticed in that direction. After putting some distance between themselves and Morelos, they would double back and head toward the road southwest of town.

"This old roan still packing you around?" asked Corbett. Joe had gone over to look at Blue's feet and to saddle up.

"Yup. Figure he's got a few years left. Good blood. Don't break 'em too early. Let 'em run for the first few years— makes for a good horse."

"That it does. I'll tell you, Joe, there'll be a helluva need for horses down here before long. Already is. Stages, ranches, the army. If you decide to leave your place after all this, you ought to drift down here. We'd have all the horse business we could handle."

"Thanks, Thad. Way I figure it, I'll either get my place back and clear things up, else I'll take down a few Milstead boys, maybe some others. Then I'll be on the run for sure."

"Cheer up, Joey. Don't sound like you to be so dead serious. Hell, we'll probably get there and find out that the law has rounded up and jailed that bunch and cleared you of the whole thing."

"Sorry." Joe threw saddle blanket and saddle over Blue's back. "Guess I'm just tired of fightin' folks."

"It's like I said the other day, Joe. This country is changing. Plenty of good people just now coming in, wanting to settle. Up till now, only the wild, young boys or the hard cases like me, would come out to a land like this. But you've got the right idea. There's a good living to be made for the man who will work hard and knows what to do. Better life than you'd have back in Mississippi. But you've got to wait a while yet for the law to come and settle things down. Meantime, you manage the best you can."

"Corbett, we'll have to get this freighter moving." It was

Blake Sutter. "Some of my customers may be coming in soon."

"Okay, Blake," said Corbett, "and I want you to know, we appreciate your help with this."

Sutter waved a hand at him. "Let's just hurry up and get out of here."

Joe finished with the gelding and walked with Corbett over to the wagon. The rest of the group was gathered around. Everything appeared ready. The wagon was stacked with bags of dirt and wooden crates such that the men could remain concealed during the ride and then shoot without being exposed.

Thad Corbett approached the saloon keeper, Van Brooks, who was talking with Scandal and Andersen. He gave them some last-minute instructions, then motioned to José Valero, who was standing off alone with his mount.

"We'll be moving out, José. Come on over and meet Joe Trento."

Valero was a short, stout young Mexican with a serious countenance. He and Joe exchanged nods, then the three retrieved their mounts and headed for the barn door.

A painted sky east of town revealed the coming of dawn. The threesome rode into the shadowy scrub land north of Morelos. They rode in silence, each man enjoying his own thoughts. Nighthawks skimmed low over the arid ground, looking for their nests or chasing a final insect before the coming of day. The day birds began to peep and chirp, but became silent again as the men passed.

Rocks, thought Joe. The land here was nothing but rocks. Multihued and pretty in the morning light, but nothing compared to the fertile delta farmland of his boyhood or even the waving seas of grass in Kansas. Joe had thought that his own mountainous land was a sparse land for grazing, yet compared to these southern deserts and basins, his mountains were truly verdant.

But Thad Corbett said people were coming . . . or at least passing through. That would mean business and prosperity for those smart enough to grab it. Corbett was right. Joe knew cattle; he had land. He would do well, very well. But only if he stayed alive and out of jail.

A wave of anxiety flowed back over Joe Trento, returning from wherever it had hidden for the last few days. When he had ridden out to Corbett's place and resigned himself to helping out with the job, he had somehow relaxed and put his original mission out of his mind.

After all, had he expected Corbett to be lying around with nothing to do? Of course the gunman had his own business to tend to. Joe should feel lucky that Corbett would be able to help him at all. But now, thinking of his ranch, Joe felt anxious and guilty. The peaceful morning ride was spoiled for him.

"Let's cut south now," said Corbett. "We're far enough from town. It's a bit of a rough climb, but it'll be worse further on. At the top of that ridge we'll be able to spot the road, I reckon. Then we'll figure a way to shadow the wagon."

"You reckon the gang is already watching?" asked Joe.

"There's a good chance of it," replied Corbett. "There are Mexicans enough in Morelos . . . I'm sure some of them are Deligro's men on the lookout for likely travelers. If not that, they most likely have someone watching the road much of the time. Every small party that has come in or out of Morelos these past few months has seen something of the gang—even you, Joe, coming down that old hog trail."

"Figure they'll hit us early?" asked Joe.

"Maybe. But these boys don't seem to care so much for an early-morning raid. They hit at midday, afternoon—anytime."

As the sun climbed, gray clouds moved in from the west.

The three horses twisted and lurched their way to the top of a craggy ridge. Corbett stopped the group.

Overhead the grayness moved across to blot out the sun, as if to say "Enough, today the land will have some relief from the scorching rays." The coolness of the night had not yet burned away, and a mild breeze had sprung up. Each man gave an inward sigh of relief. This would make the difference between a hot, torturous ride and a relatively comfortable one.

The three dismounted and continued on foot, squatting low as they neared the top. Indeed, the road from Morelos was visible in the distance. The decline fell away more gently than the side they had just scaled, forming a shallow valley through which the road ran, about a half mile off, barely noticeable among the drab landscape. The men might have actually overlooked it, except that there was the freight wagon, traveling along, almost out of sight!

"Let's move, boys!" said Corbett. The three scrambled to the horses and mounted. They half trotted, half slid back down to relatively flat ground, then turned and cantered toward the northwest. The ridge was on their left, separating them from the valley through which the road ran.

"I'll ride back up and have another look soon," Corbett called over the hoofbeats. "The valley curves northward up ahead and so does the road. You two cut across and head for that little pass. Wait for me there." Corbett pointed and Joe and José looked. Indeed, the ridge that separated them from the wagon road curved gently northward, and there was a small saddle in it several miles away. By cutting across, they would be able to reach that spot well before the wagon. Joe and Valero hauled on their reins and hightailed it across the open plain.

"Hell, they could be attacked anytime," Valero yelled.

"I reckon so," called Joe. "Carter and Brooks must have started too soon—or else we poked along mighty slow."

Several minutes later they were again climbing the ridge, and again they stopped a short distance from the top. This time Joe could plainly see the road following a small river that ran through the center of the valley. The wagon was just rounding the curve to the south, and all seemed well.

"I don't see any trouble," said Joe.

"Turn aroun', *señor,*" said an accented voice, "and you will see *mucho* trouble then."

CHAPTER 11

A CHILL RAN down Joe's spine. He turned slowly and looked into the gun barrels of five of the fiercest looking men he had ever seen!

"Howdy," Joe said, attempting a smile. "No need to hold those rifles on us, *amigos*. We're just waitin' for some friends down below." He instantly cursed himself for revealing the presence of the wagon.

"You think I am stupid, gringo?" said an outlaw. "Why have you run so hard to sneak up on your 'friends'?"

He appeared to be the leader of the group—the oldest, biggest, and fattest, with a gruesome scar running across his greasy face, as though it had been cleft with a sword years before.

"We are not sneaking," said Valero. "Just trying to catch up to them, that is all."

"That is not what I think," said another. "I think you are *ladrones*, like us . . . very bad men." The group broke into laughter.

"No," said the leader, "maybe they are *banditos* like us . . . but they are not nearly so bad." They laughed again, even louder.

Damn, thought Joe. How could they have been so foolish? Naturally, anyone up on the ridge would have spotted them dashing madly across the open as they had. They should have planned more carefully . . . stayed out of sight.

The boss spoke to one of his men in Spanish, and the man stepped over to Joe. He bent down and jerked Joe's revolver out of its holster, and also picked up the rifle lying nearby. He crossed to Valero and did the same.

"Listen, *amigos*," said Joe, "how about letting us go down to our people. We don't want a fight—"

"There will be no fight, gringo," said the boss, "because you have nothing to fight with!" The outlaws threw their heads back for a third time and howled with laughter.

"Unfortunately," the fat man continued, "there is no place here for another bunch of *banditos* besides us, but do not worry. We will take good care of your friends for you." As he spoke, he stepped over to Joe, who was still on the ground. He stood with his carbine resting over a beefy shoulder, a thick hand gripping the barrel. Suddenly, he raised the gun overhead to bludgeon Joe.

The rifle swung downward with surprising speed, aimed for Joe's head. Instead of cringing helplessly, Joe rolled into the outlaw and kicked his attacker behind the calf. The rifle butt thudded into the dirt and the big man's legs flew out from under him. He landed hard on his back with a roar of anger.

For a moment his companions were too stunned to react. Then they, too, rushed forward with rifles raised, one with a machete drawn.

Joe and José rolled and scrambled; Joe expected to have his skull crushed at any moment.

A shot rang out and an outlaw dropped! The others turned, bewildered. Another shot—another down! A third jerked his rifle up and aimed downhill. Joe took two steps and launched himself through the air, hitting the man as his rifle cracked! They fell and rolled down the incline.

Joe grabbed the front of the bandit's shirt and slammed an elbow into his face. The man grunted in pain, but hooked a right to the side of Joe's head. Joe partially blocked the hook, came up astride the other, and finished him with several smashing blows.

Joe glanced up at the ridge. Valero had scooped up a rifle and was holding it on the fat man and his remaining companion. Boots crunched on the gravel and Joe's head whipped around. There stood a grinning Thaddeus Corbett, rifle in hand.

"Damn you, Corbett! What's the idea running us right smack into the gang? We're the ones supposed to be getting the jump on them!"

"Calm down, Joey!" Corbett laughed. "They're just a scouting party. Sorry for the scare, though. C'mon, we need to have a look up top."

Joe disarmed the Mexican who was now coming to. He marched the prisoner back up to Valero and the others.

"I've talked to plenty of prospectors coming in from this direction," said Corbett, "the ones who were robbed by these fellows and were lucky enough to live to tell about it. The gang usually attacks from the south side of the road . . . That's why I figured we were safe over here on the north side."

They crawled the last few feet to the top of the ridge and peered over. There was the wagon, poking along like before. Andersen and Brooks appeared calm from this distance. The two shots, heard from afar, must not have alarmed them.

"You can see that the land to the south breaks up quicker than on our side," said Corbett. "That makes for better cover—a better place for an attack. Most of the trouble has been right along here, so we need to move."

The captives were bound and left sitting against a large rock. Corbett, Joe, and Valero moved out, leading the outlaws' ponies behind them. This time, however, they stayed higher up in the rubble and picked their way slowly through a maze of giant boulders and vicious cacti. Periodically, they paused to climb up and check for the wagon.

The day wore on. Joe worried that the men they had left behind were originally supposed to notify the main party of any potential victims moving down the road. Without word from their scouts, the rest of the gang might doze peacefully in some shady canyon while the wagon passed by unnoticed and the trap would have failed.

Or perhaps there was no major detachment of Deligro's gang in the area at all. They were known to roam widely at times; perhaps they had caught wind of a desirable stagecoach or shipment of some sort a hundred miles from Morelos. If there were no more outlaws about, or if Corbett had misjudged their habits, the wagon might continue clear to Tucson without incident. Joe was anxious to get this job done so he could get back to the situation in San Martin.

The trio was having an easy enough time keeping up with the wagon, so Corbett decided to stop and rest the animals. José Valero pointed out a small, almost imperceptible patch of green several hundred yards downhill. Upon investigation, the group found a large, flat rock, several dozen feet in diameter, half buried in the hillside along with the usual rubble. The stone was positioned in such a way that it gathered a large portion of the rainfall running down that section of the slope. The water then flowed toward the center of the slab, where there was a slight depression, then ran off to form a shallow pool when the stone disappeared into the earth. Judging by the patterns on the ground, this little pool overflowed and streamed downhill during rainy weather, perhaps forming a seasonal rivulet somewhere in the land below, similar to the small river flowing through the valley behind them.

The important fact, however, was that the pool still held moisture now, a permanent enough supply to support a few water-loving shrubs, and, judging by the numerous tracks, quite a few of the local varmints.

"This is a fine spot, José," said Corbett. "We can take ten minutes here and give these ponies a rest. One of us will have to go up and watch the wagon, though."

"I'll go," said Joe. "My legs could use some limbering up." Hours in the saddle, day after day, could make a man's legs stiff and weak. The climb would be good, and Joe was too agitated to sit still anyway.

Joe Trento lay on his belly and stared blankly at the valley just as he had already done a dozen times that day. The wagon was there. It had stopped in the shade of a huge, lonely tree. Their horses must have needed a rest, too, Joe guessed. The men hiding in the back of the wagon probably were having a rough time of it stuffed in as they were under phony sacks of merchandise. Fortunately, it was still overcast and a decent breeze was blowing—a rare blessing. Usually it would be sunny and blistering hot by now.

The ride had strung out longer than anyone had anticipated. Andersen and Brooks had stepped down to stretch their legs.

A movement—a mile away—caught Joe's attention. His eyes scanned the area, searching for the thing his brain told him was wrong. There it was again! A darting shape . . . moving, then stopping. Moving again.

Joe crawled backward on his stomach until he was below the line of the ridge. Then he stood and leapt downhill to the others. Corbett and Valero looked up.

"They're comin'!" Joe said.

"You sure?"

"I'm sure. Someone's workin' down through the brush. Looks like the river's only a few inches deep—a few yards across. They could make a run and be on 'em in no time— and the wagon's stopped. Andersen's resting the horses."

"Damn!" said Corbett. He and José scrambled to their feet. All three mounted, and urged the animals straight up the slope.

"We've got problems," said Corbett, looking down at the road. "I'd planned on the action takin' place in the open, with the wagon on the move. The river has cut close to the far side just there. . . . The bastards can sneak to within a few feet of our boys. They'll be wiped out before they know it."

Joe saw what Corbett meant. Although the little river generally meandered through the center of the valley, due to some quirk in the lay of the land, it had angled over to the far side for a spell.

"We need to warn them," said Valero.

"Right," said Corbett. "José, you and Joe have to make those ponies of yours cover some ground. Head north for a ways, then cut clear across. If the shooting starts, you might not be noticed. Put your spurs into those cayuses and get across pronto. Then start workin' back south and we'll have Deligro from both sides."

"What'll you do?" asked Joe.

"You'll see in a minute." Corbett spurred his horse over the precipice. For a moment, Joe thought both horse and rider would surely tumble head over heels and be dashed against the rocks below, but the big sorrel leapt and slid and managed to stay on its feet. Then the ground leveled out a bit, and Corbett spurred the horse into a flat-out gallop. He pulled his six-gun and blasted six quick shots into the air, accompanied by a shrieking war cry.

Carter Andersen moved with amazing quickness for a man of his bulk. He was on his feet and halfway to the wagon before Van Brooks had started to rise. In a minute, they would realize that it was not one of Deligro's men coming at them, but for now they were lashing the team into a mad dash down the road, which was what Corbett wanted.

Corbett was also counting on the Mexicans to make their move momentarily. It would take him another minute or two to overtake the group; if the bandits were in the rocks on the other side, they'd move to attack the wagon before it got out of sight. They'd also move to stop him from interfering.

Joe and Valero found a trail just below the rim of the

ridge. They raced along at a hard gallop, weaving and ducking among the jagged outcroppings and gnarled limbs. They'd traveled almost a mile when shots sounded from over the ridge . . . first just a few, then a half dozen, finally a continuous outpouring of pistol and rifle fire.

"Now!" shouted Joe. He reined his gelding sharply off of the trail and up over the crest. He and Valero imitated Corbett's wild ride down the valley wall, save that they fired no shots.

Onto the flat plain they raced. Andersen had driven the big freighter across the river and into cover on the far side. Several of the men had spilled out and taken up positions among the rocks. The others stayed in the vehicle, firing from behind the sacks of dirt.

Andersen's move, although not in the plan, was a good one. The Mexicans had raced out into the open valley to give chase to what they thought were defenseless townsfolk. Instead of continuing to flee, Andersen had taken advantage of some good cover, allowing his men to pour a huge volley of lead into the outlaws, who were without significant cover themselves.

Joe and Valero would pass several hundred yards north of the battle. The bandits might spy them and spoil the element of surprise, but at this distance they'd be safe from fire.

Their horses slowed as the land began to rise to the far valley wall. They urged their mounts well up the incline before dismounting.

They crept southward until they found a suitable spot for observation. The wagon was somewhat sheltered by a huge pile of flat stones. Wade Scandal and his men were out and firing from behind the rocks. Carter Andersen and Van Brooks had also made their way several feet uphill, where they were concealed in a small gully.

That left Andersen's two men and Sutter in the wagon, firing slowly and methodically at the valley below. All of their group, Joe noted, had the advantage of height and view over the outlaws.

Joe could see the Mexicans here and there, well spread out, twenty-five to fifty yards away. Some were dead and dotted the river bank in plain sight; others had taken refuge behind what brush or other cover they could find.

A few had managed to make it to the sloping valley wall, and Joe guessed that some had given up and made their escape over the western ridge. Joe and his companion assessed the scene a moment longer, noting the locations of the cutthroats by the puffs of smoke from their firearms.

Valero spotted one such puff much farther out in the valley. He nudged Joe and pointed. "Corbett," he said. Corbett had apparently abandoned his horse and begun pecking away at the gang from a low spot far beyond the river. The sorrel was nowhere in sight.

The two began to stalk southward again. Their intent was to arrive at a point on the valley wall directly above the outlaws. They were careful, however, to keep their guns at the ready, since some of Deligro's gang might be fleeing up the incline.

They passed above the wagon and looked down upon Andersen and Brooks, hidden in the gully only fifty yards below. The rancher and saloon keeper were too busy firing at the gang to notice Joe and Valero passing by above.

Suddenly Joe heard voices—low, angry words, spoken in Spanish. He motioned to Valero and the two lowered themselves to their bellies and crept over the stones. The sight that greeted them froze their hearts.

Seven or eight of the outlaws crouched against a boulder, heavily armed and looking mean. Apparently, this group had reacted quickly when the wagon opened fire and had made it up into the rocks. The outlaws intended to flank and wipe out the wagon just as Trento hoped to flank the outlaws.

One man commented bitterly to the others, then motioned for them to follow. The band moved out directly toward Joe and Valero.

Joe loathed to shoot a man, even an outlaw, without warning, but too much was at stake to take any chances. He nodded to Valero, and the two silently raised their carbines.

Each man took an outlaw in the chest with his first shot. Valero's marksmanship served them well, as his rifle continued to bark, downing two more. Joe's second and third shots missed. He cursed softly. He would have made those shots with a handgun. He aimed at a fierce, mustachioed face charging toward him with pistols blazing. Trento's rifle cracked; the man tumbled forward and died.

Another was scrambling upward, trying to get above the duo. Valero aimed swiftly and fired, and the man fell head over heels, back toward the valley floor. A seventh man had retreated and disappeared into the rocks.

An uneasy silence hung over the valley. The shooting had suddenly stopped. Joe raised himself up, rifle ready, and looked around.

A wispy haze of gunsmoke hung over the area, evidence of the amount of gunfire there had been. There was no movement on the valley floor.

They heard voices coming from the wagon. Joe called, and Carter Andersen answered with a shout.

"Hold your positions," Joe yelled. "Some of these fellows may still be around out here." Andersen yelled back an acknowledgment.

Slowly, with ready carbines, Joe and Valero continued their trek. After traveling another fifty yards, they turned and descended.

The bodies of the murderous gang lay strewn here and there. They had tried to take cover behind the scant brush, but it had afforded little protection. Valero walked backward, keeping his eyes trained on the craggy hillside they had just left.

Joe approached a body, verified that it was dead, moved on to the next. All told, ten men lay dead by the little river; not one was found still breathing. Thad Corbett had hoped to take a big bite out of Deligro's outlaws; he had gotten his wish. Including the five men previously encountered on the eastern rim, the seven Joe and José had attacked in the rocks, and the unknown number who had escaped, the raiding party must have totaled over two dozen men.

Joe heard a long "halloo" and looked up to see Corbett approaching through the brush.

"All dead." said Joe. "I've counted ten here."

"Fine job, Joey," said Corbett, looking tired. "Let's see how the rest of our bunch made out." Together they made their way to the others.

The men were rising from their positions and stretching cramped muscles. Carter Andersen had been shot in the arm as he was jumping from the wagon. One of Andersen's men, who had remained in the vehicle, was hit in the hand. Otherwise, the group had not suffered a scratch.

"I'd say we've been powerful lucky," said Corbett. "I'll admit, when I looked down and saw the fighting clear over on this side . . . I looked for some bad trouble."

Joe told the group of his and Valero's short battle with the seven up on the hillside.

"I'll be damned," said Corbett. "Joey, I guess I owe you and José a debt. Not only did you save us all from an ambush, you two have gone and captured the deadliest outlaw west of New Orleans."

"How's that?" Joe asked.

"The fat man you've got tied up over on the other side . . . that's Carlos Deligro."

CHAPTER 12

JOE, CORBETT, AND Valero started out two mornings later. Corbett had paid Joe the cut he had been promised. He also insisted that Joe and Valero split the reward that was offered for the capture of Deligro. The money was more than Valero would make in six months working for the local Anglo ranchers. They were difficult bosses, especially tough on Mexicans—and so Valero decided to accept Joe's offer to ride north and back Corbett and him against the Milsteads.

Not to get yourself killed, Joe had explained, just be an extra gun, even up the odds if necessary. He had told him he could cut out anytime he wanted to, but he had also offered an enticing incentive for the young man. If things went well, Valero could buy into Joe's ranch like Al Grundy had.

Valero had jumped at the opportunity. And he didn't mind the notion of riding with Joe and Corbett on another adventure.

For his part, Joe Trento had developed a liking for the Mexican. He was quiet, smart, and effective. There was plenty of land if Valero decided to run some stock of his own. It was worth sacrificing some of his ranch to get another fighting man. The success of his ranch, Joe now believed, depended on his ability to defend it and his other possessions from tactics like those of the Milstead family. Joe was relieved to finally be on his way back—and with two formidable companions alongside.

On each hip rode a fancy Colt revolver, impressive replacements for the old gun of Marshal Josh Parker that

Joe had been using. These had belonged to Carlos Deligro himself and had been awarded to Joe by the citizens of Morelos. Joe felt better with the newer, more powerful weapons.

He had been thinking about Corbett's comments regarding their strategy. Corbett had said that the main thing was to get back on his land . . . let the law and the Milsteads seek him out if they so wished. Joe could see the sense in this. Originally he had envisioned himself, along with Corbett, riding smack into town, blasting away at any Milsteads they saw, and somehow setting everything straight. Now, after some reflection, Joe saw the wisdom of Corbett's way.

The country was full of outlaws, feuding settlers, and pistol-packing cowboys. Most lawmen would not have the time or ambition to spare for tracking down a possible wrongdoer who was currently minding his own business, and perhaps time, along with the exposure of the devious ways of the Milsteads, would fade the memory of Joe's alleged crime in the minds of the townsfolk.

The Milsteads themselves might be more difficult to hide from, but that was why Corbett and José Valero were along.

Still, Joe knew he would never feel right until he was officially cleared of the murder charge. It had been over a week since he had busted out of jail. The marshal of San Martin was dead. A circuit judge may or may not have appeared. If he had, he may or may not have been able to bring any real law and order to the town. The deputy, Billy Heywood, was undoubtedly struggling with the issue of the marshal's murder. Plenty of folks must have witnessed the shooting, so there would be no doubt as to the guilty party. Unfortunately, the people the Milsteads had gathered to lynch Joe were not of the caliber to stand behind the deputy, ready to fight the Milsteads.

Joe tapped his heels against the blue roan's sides and

trotted up between Valero and Corbett. They were several hours from Morelos, retracing Joe's trail from Maysville.

"Say, Thad, I've been thinking about a plan," said Joe. Corbett raised his eyebrows. Joe continued, "When we get up north, I figure we ought to head for the ranch—dodge the town like you said. But before anyone knows we're back, there's one thing I'd like to do."

"What's that, Joey?"

"Well, I sure would like to sneak over to where that Shorty feller was killed. Even if I can't find the exact spot, maybe there'll be some sign of what really happened."

"What sort of sign?"

"I don't know. I just know that I won't rest easy until I check around a bit."

"Can't blame you, Joe. A murder charge is a helluva thing to live with, even if the law doesn't get on you for it. I suppose a little look-see wouldn't be a bad idea. Then," Corbett went on, "I still think you need to get back to your *rancho*, back to work and all, but there's some other information we'll need."

"What do you mean?"

"This is your show, Joe. José and I are here to back you, but it seems to me that we have to know what sort of fix that town is in. You know, are those Milsteads still out free or are they jailed, is the deputy in control of things, are they lookin' for you, that sort of thing."

"How do you aim to find out?"

"I'll go in. They won't know me, won't know we're together. You and José can keep low up at your place and I'll trot down for a beer or two."

Joe agreed. He wasn't sure what all this poking around would reveal, but he felt better just having some plans in place.

The loafers in front of the Maysville cantina stood up in alarm as three riders appeared in the haze. Joe, Corbett, and Valero could have been some of Deligro's men, judging by their appearance.

The loafers tried to appear nonchalant as they strolled off. The three men dismounted and tied up in front of the cantina.

Lupita Sanchez also looked worried when the men clomped through the door until she recognized Corbett and Joe. Then, she broke into a wide grin.

"Corbett!" she called out. She walked around from behind the bar.

"Lupita!" Corbett called with a laugh. He gave her a friendly squeeze.

Joe glanced around the room. A mirror behind the bar was broken. A smashed table leaned in a corner. Joe spied a half-dozen bullet holes in the ceiling.

"You found your friend," said the girl to Joe, "and another one as well." She looked up at Valero and blushed.

"I'll tell you," said Joe Trento, "he was in Morelos like you said, but it took some hunting to flush him out. This here is José Valero."

"And they both go with you to your *rancho*? But you must stay for a while—until tomorrow at least. Pablo will like to talk with you."

"How is old Pablo?" Corbett asked. "Keepin' his nose clean?" They sat down wearily at a table. Joe noticed a group of men at the bar looking their way. He recognized some of them from his last visit.

"Things are not so good for him," said Lupita. "He is still having trouble with the men."

"What kind of trouble?" asked Corbett.

"Pablo is a good man," explained the girl. "He is the only good young man here. The rest are drunks and thieves, hired hands and drifters . . . who knows? This is such a little place that there is no one to stand up to them. Pablo works for *Señor* Rodriguez and some of the other merchants here. He feels like he must protect us from the abuse. Usually he gets beaten up . . . I am afraid he will be killed."

"Where is he now?" asked Corbett.

"Over at White's—the dry goods store."

"See what kind of grub you can find us, will you? And beer too, then go tell Pablo we're here—if he doesn't already know. Maybe we can cheer him up."

Lupita smiled and left.

"This little place could start to do some business soon," continued Corbett, "if the scum don't ruin it first."

Lupita returned and the men ate and drank, enjoying the coolness of the cantina after the hot ride.

Presently, a smiling Pablo came striding through the doors and gave a loud whoop at the sight of Corbett and Joe.

"*Amigos,* how good to see you again. I am glad you found each other. Now I have my two favorite customers here at the same time . . . and their companion too." He was eyeing Valero, sizing him up.

"It's good to see you too, Pablo," said Corbett. "This here's José Valero. He's going with us to help Joe out."

"You must stay tonight," said Pablo. "We can find you a place—and get you a few good meals before you leave."

"Reckon we'll stay the night. Our ponies been ridden hard lately . . . but we'll camp nearby. No roof for us."

"I would insist," said the gracious Pablo, "if I did not know how you cowboys love the stars—but I will take your horses and see to them."

"Sit down first," said Joe, "and visit while we finish our grub."

Pablo dragged a chair across the sawdust and straddled it backward. "Lupita will make something better than this in the morning. Rodriguez made this."

"Tastes fine to me," Joe said. Just then the rough-looking group at the bar tossed down the last of their drinks and walked out, eyeballing the four at the table.

"Say," said Corbett, "Lupita tells us these boys around here are still locking horns with you. What's up?"

The smile disappeared from Pablo's face. "These *perros*," he said, "they think they own this town. They have no honor. They will strike a woman or an old man for amusement. When they get drunk, I get in the way so they strike me instead, but"—he shrugged—"there are many of them and they have guns. I am only one and know nothing of pistols."

"I know what you're trying to do, Pablo," said Corbett, "but you're making a mistake. Eventually, these boys will kill you. If you want my opinion, you'd best quit messing with them or else learn to fight on their terms. And that means shooting."

"But I just told you, *amigo,* I cannot shoot. I have tried before and I am very bad. I would rather fight them with my fists."

"Pablo, I've seen men like these before, and they're always the same. They wear guns, and they're good with them. They're loud and tough sounding. But you'd be surprised how many are cowards. It's easy for them to fight you in here—they've got their buddies and the stakes are low—but if they were lookin' down a gun barrel . . . well, most are just pups."

"What do you think I should do?"

"Well, I'm not sure. I'd hate for you to get shot, *amigo,* but I think you're headed for worse the way things are going now."

Joe wondered what Thad was up to. Nothing that would delay their trip northward, he hoped. "Isn't there anyone else in town who will talk back to these rattlesnakes?" he asked.

"Colin, perhaps," said Pablo, "the gunsmith—he does not like Prescott and his bunch—and perhaps Rodriguez, whose place this is. He lets the men drink here, but gets angry at their abuse." Joe recalled that Prescott was the name of the man he had hit with the chair.

"Let's go see this fellow Colin," said Corbett suddenly. "I was going to suggest a visit with him anyway."

Sean Colin emerged from his back room, wiping his hands on a cloth. He made a decent living as Maysville's gunsmith, but he was a man with insight and realized that he stood to profit even more if the town were chosen as a trading center by the increasing number of range seekers and settlers moving through. Therefore, like Rodriguez, he was upset with the reputation that Maysville seemed to be acquiring as a haven for thieves and drifters. He walked eagerly toward Pablo and the three strangers, anticipating some business.

"Evening, gentleman," he said pleasantly. "And how can I help you?"

"*Señor* Colin," said Pablo, "this is *Señor* Corbett . . . you have heard me talk of him." Pablo looked up, embarrassed. He didn't know how to continue. Corbett jumped in.

"Nice to meet you, Mister Colin. You might say we're sort of regulars over at the cantina. Just passing through, though. Mister Trento here has land up around San Martin, and my home is mainly in Morelos, but our business takes us through Maysville now and then. Nice little town."

"I think so, too," said Sean Colin, "and I hope it stays that way. Good deal of trouble lately, though."

"How's that?" Corbett asked.

"Right now, I figure this town has got equal parts decent folk and bums, if you know what I mean. If more honest folk settle, the place will grow—be a real nice little town. If they don't, well, we'll just stay a one-horse town full of saloons and whorehouses, if that. Lately, those who come through usually get scared off by that bunch over there." He indicated the cantina with a nod.

"Pablo here and his pretty little cousin have been sayin'

something similar," replied Corbett. "Seems to me, folks like you could get together and do something about it."

Joe and José Valero ambled off in different directions, examining racks of rifles and revolvers. Joe pretended to ignore the conversation.

"Mister, we're mighty poor, most of us," said Colin. "No cash money around to hire a lawman. Hell, half the time I'm paid in chickens or vegetables. If you're a gun lookin' for a job, you're in the wrong place."

"I'm not," said Corbett, glancing around the shop, "but obviously there are plenty of guns in town already."

"I see what you mean." The gunsmith looked over Corbett, Trento, and Valero, one by one. "You're a tough-looking lot yourselves—no offense, mind you—what I mean is, most of the men in Maysville have families. Passels of kids, most of 'em. It ain't easy to raise any sort of vigilante group."

"Got any decent scatterguns?"

Joe grinned. Old Thaddeus was like a bulldog, once he got hold of an idea.

The gunsmith stared blankly a moment. "I've got a few." He turned to the rack. "Here you go," he said, turning back. "It's not new, but it's a fine shotgun. Bore's good. I've been over it myself. Five dollars."

Corbett looked over the weapon only briefly. "Done," he said, digging in his pocket for the cash. "And some shells too, while you're at it."

Sean Colin was pleased. He hurried off to get the ammunition, forgetting the conversation for a moment. He returned quickly and stacked four boxes on the countertop. Corbett gathered them up.

"Mister," said Corbett, "I don't mean to stick my nose in where it don't belong. It's none of my business how this town handles its affairs, and it's not my place to send anyone out to get in a shootin' match, either. On the other hand, I've been through a dozen little towns like this one after the riffraff got through with them. That's when the folks call on me. Usually a few boys like Pablo here have already died. I'm just telling you what I've seen, that's all. It's been a pleasure doin' business."

Sean Colin said nothing as the four walked out.

"*Señor* Corbett, what do you want with a shotgun?" asked Pablo.

"Come on out while we make camp, and I'll show you."

"Let me tell Rodriguez." Pablo headed across the street to the cantina.

"Look for us by the river," Corbett called, "and bring something for these ponies."

As the three men mounted and started out of town, they could hear laughter and shouting emanating from the little saloon. The boys were getting fired up for the evening.

CHAPTER 13

JOE AND JOSÉ squatted by a tiny fire, tending a pot of coffee. Pablo Orazco stood with Corbett a couple of dozen yards off.

"A pistol is not really such a good weapon for most men," Corbett was saying. "When you've got trouble, what you want is a long gun . . . and you want it pointing at the other man before he has a chance to draw." The shotgun roared as Pablo blasted off the last of a tattered cloth that Corbett had tied to an unfortunate cottonwood branch. After the first few misses and some instruction from the old master, the young man had fired five times and had hit his mark five times.

"This is nothing like shooting a pistol," said Pablo. "I have hunted with my father long ago, but I had forgotten the feel of shooting such a gun."

"Like I said, the handgun is a difficult weapon. It's good because it's small and can be carried easily, but that's about it. You take this shotgun, boy. You may decide that you need it, or you may not—"

"I cannot, *amigo*!" Pablo tried to thrust the gun back at Corbett. "I could never pay you for it!"

Corbett was in no mood to argue. "All right, but you have to keep it for a spell. I'm taking my rifle and the rest of my gear up to Joe's already. I can't pack a scatter gun too, can I? You keep it here and I'll fetch it on my way back."

Hoofbeats pounded over the rise, and the squatting men jumped to their feet. Lupita galloped over the knoll, bareback, astride a small pony. She slid to a stop almost on top of the fire.

"They think you have left town," she gasped. "They started hitting *Señor* Rodriguez—"

"Slow down," said Joe. "Who's hitting who?"

"The same bunch. Prescott and those *perros*. They think Rodriguez called you to frighten them. Please hurry! I am afraid they will kill him!"

Corbett and Pablo had walked over in time to hear Lupita's statements.

"José," Corbett said, "stay with the camp. Someone may be watching us." Joe and Corbett threw saddles onto their horses and headed out at a gallop.

The horses pounded over the turf until the rear of the cantina appeared in the night. As the two approached they slowed to a quiet trot, then a walk, hoping that they would not be heard by those inside.

They dismounted and entered a back storeroom. All was quiet. Joe crossed the space and peered through a partially open door leading to the front. His eyes swept the room, seeing no one, until they came to the limp body of Rodriguez, slumped unconscious over his own bar. The cowards had beaten the old man senseless, and then fled, Joe thought. He pushed the door open with a curse and bolted toward the old man.

Something stirred behind the bar! Joe leapt, spinning, reaching for a gun.

A shot boomed and Joe's shoulder burned. His own pistol roared and shattered bottles behind the bar. Joe hit the ground and fanned off two more shots. "Corbett, a trap! Get out!" he yelled.

Instead, the old *pistolero* kicked open the door and stepped through. He worked his lever action and sprayed the room with fire.

Joe scrambled to his feet, but bullets whizzed close to his head and he dove again between the tables and chairs. He looked up in time to see Thad Corbett crumple to the ground, struck from behind.

Joe groaned, half in pain, half in despair. Once again a gunfight . . . trouble.

"Now, boy," said a voice, "show us how a big-time gun-slinger handles himself!"

Joe looked up at one of the bums from the saloon. A second one stepped up beside him. They pointed rifles at Joe's chest.

"He ain't so tough in a real fight," said the latter, "when he don't have a chance for no fancy draw!"

"He got Archie!" someone called. Joe remembered the man behind the bar.

"Is he dead?"

"Nope. Out cold, though."

"Take him to the shack," ordered another voice. It sounded familiar. Joe twisted and saw Prescott standing over Corbett who was starting to come to.

"We'll help these two back out to their camp," said Prescott. " 'Course, no tellin' what sort of accident might happen along the way."

The other men smirked. Eight of Prescott's crew were involved in the fight; all were now milling about, inspecting the captives.

"Get up, old man," said Prescott. "Let's see if you're as tough as your rep." He kicked Corbett hard in the ribs.

"Enough! Touch him again and I will kill you!"

Pablo! All heads turned toward the front. There he was, leaning around the front door . . . pointing the shotgun.

Damn! This was the last person Joe wanted involved. Tough-enough fix for Corbett and him—it would be worse having to look out for the boy.

The men in the bar scattered at the sight of the big gun. They took up positions behind the bar and under tables, pointing their weapons toward the front.

The boy would be blown to pieces. Someone was proba-

bly sneaking out the back door already! The only hope
was the fact that the men inside had fairly poor cover. If
shooting started, Pablo might get some of them before he
went down. This knowledge would cause anyone sneaking
around outside to hesitate.

Prescott, unlike the others, hadn't jumped for cover. He
stood over Corbett, pointing a barrel at the semiconscious
gunman. A groan came from Rodriguez.

"Don't be a fool, boy," shouted Prescott. "You shoot at
us and we'll kill your friends!"

"Move away, Prescott," shouted Pablo. "Let both of them
go."

A rifle cracked outside! Pablo shot a glance over his
shoulder but didn't budge. He shouted something across
the street. Someone was backing him!

"Listen, boy," said Prescott, "we've got no quarrel with
you. It's these hired guns we're after. We can't have this
scum taking over Maysville, can we?"

Joe saw a shadow in the back room, directly behind
Prescott. Lupita? God, he hoped not. Then the gunsmith
stepped through the door!

He held a huge, old Colt Walker in his hand. "Put up
the rifle, Prescott, or I'll kill you."

Prescott stiffened, afraid to turn around. "Colin? That
you? What the hell! You stickin' up for this scum too?"

"We've had enough of you and your bunch," said Sean
Colin. "Put up the rifle or I'll shoot you in the back—I
swear it!"

Joe was still prone on the floor, but he had his guns and
plenty of shots left. He wondered who he should go for.

"You'll be killed, Colin . . . my boys will cut you down."

"I doubt it. That scattergun will take out half of 'em,
and I'll get *you*! Besides, the girl's gone for her folks—kin
to Rodriguez and the boy there. You'll never get out alive,
unless you give up!"

"The hell I will!" Prescott said, sneering. He spun

swiftly. The older man didn't have the speed of Hal Prescott, but he didn't need it. As the rifle barrel neared his face, Colin's huge revolver roared. Prescott flew back in a cloud of smoke.

Instantly, a tall, skinny cardsharp drew quickly and aimed at Pablo, but Trento's gun sounded first, and the man spun across the bar!

Pablo let go with the shotgun, filling the cantina with a deafening boom. Another man went down, and the rest dove to the floor. The shotgun roared again, and the drifters twisted and crawled, looking for better cover. Colin, Trento, and Pablo had all fired in rapid succession, soundling like a weird Gatling gun.

"Don't shoot!" someone shouted. "Don't shoot!"

"Hold your fire, Pablo!" Joe yelled. "Nobody move! Mister Colin, go round and get their guns. Pablo, stay where you are. Everyone else stay on the floor."

"I had nothing to do with it," whined a potbellied man, "Prescott—he was the one!"

"We'll see about that," Joe said.

Just then Lupita pushed past Pablo and ran to Rodriguez. Two Mexican men followed. Another, about Pablo's age, stepped through, holding an ancient carbine. Pablo spoke to him in Spanish, and the newcomer trained the gun on the room.

Joe moved toward Corbett, who was conscious now, trying to sit up. "You all right, old buddy?" Joe asked.

"What happened? I got popped from behind."

"That you did, and our gunsmith friend killed the fellow who did it."

Corbett sat up and looked around. Colin was kicking pistols and rifles into a pile in the middle of the room. Pablo and his friend were keeping a bead on everyone.

Rodriguez was being tended to, and Prescott lay dead before them.

"What the hell do we do now?" Corbett muttered.

"I dunno," replied Joe. "You're the one with all the ideas."

Groans arose from Prescott's wounded buddies. Corbett got to his feet and lurched around the room, looking. Rodriguez had been badly beaten, but would be all right. The Mexicans rushed him off to be cared for. The other wounds, including Joe's, would need attention soon, but could wait. Nothing could be done for Prescott, of course.

Outside, a surprising number of citizens had gathered in the street. Joe had not realized that there were so many Anglos in Maysville. Several merchants and cattlemen, acquaintances of Sean Colin, wandered into the room.

Corbett ordered the gang over to the wall opposite the bar, where he had them sit on the floor. Additional towns-folk came in, a few at a time, until there was quite a crowd.

Corbett addressed the captives: "You men, some of you may be innocent in all this, and I'm sorry if you are. On the other hand, old Rodriguez, looks like he'll come around, and I've a feeling he'll point out most of you as having had a hand in this—if the girl doesn't do so first. Prescott was killed in a fair fight, far as I'm concerned. The rest of you can go for the nearest law, if you've a mind to, but I don't think you will. All told, I think you can see that there are a few men in this town willing to take your heads off with a load of buckshot if you give them much more trouble. I guess that's all I've got to say."

The men on the floor grumbled, but the onlookers murmured approvingly. Sean Colin hiked up his britches a bit, cleared his throat, and stepped forward.

"Well, we been talkin' amongst ourselves here a bit— Hank and Emmett Mays and a bunch of the others—and the way we feel about it, we don't care to take any action against you men right now. One man's dead already, and that's enough. There ain't no law here, nor any judge to pass any sorta sentence, but after this, we're lookin' to hire a marshal and get some law and order here in Maysville."

"How 'bout Colin fer marshal!" someone yelled from the crowd. Sean Colin turned beet red.

A white-haired cattleman stepped up, the one Colin had called Emmett Mays. "Colin's right," he said. "This town's growing, and it's time we had a proper peace officer. This is a good town for folks who're law abidin' . . . if you're not, I advise you to get out!"

Again the crowd buzzed approvingly. Corbett motioned for the men to get up, and they slowly rose and headed to the door. The citizens parted to let them through, then broke up themselves, milling around in the cantina and out on the boardwalk.

"Thaddeus," Joe asked, "you going to stay alive long enough to take care of my business?"

"I truly hope so, Joey," Corbett said, rubbing a lump on his head. "I'm gettin' too old for these interruptions."

"We'd better get on back. José is prob'ly wonderin' where those crazy gringos rode off to."

Joe related the evening's events to José Valero while the latter bandaged Joe's shoulder by firelight.

"Corbett, why he dropped like a sack of grain," Joe teased. "He'd be sleepin' there yet if I hadn't 've gone over and gave him a nudge."

Corbett grinned and shook his head. "I just hope that's all the killin' this town has to see for a spell. I'm lookin' for these people to get together and take control of things. Leastways, that's what I hope they'll do."

The three men turned to the clip-clop of hooves. Sean Colin and Pablo Orazco appeared out of the darkness.

"Howdy, boys!" called Joe. "Come on in and set a spell." The two dismounted and squatted by the fire. Joe dipped up cups of coffee.

"Your head, Corbett," Pablo asked, "is it bad?"

"Well, yes," replied the gunman, "but this ain't the first time—prob'ly not the last neither, I'm sad to say. I guess

I'll get along. What I want to know," he continued, "is how it felt blasting away with that scattergun today. You did the right thing, boy."

"I am glad that I killed no one," said Pablo.

"So am I," replied Corbett, "but believe me, what you and Mister Colin did there this evening will head off a lot of trouble in the future. By the way, Colin, I'm obliged for what you did back there. I'da been in a sorry situation if you hadn't stepped in."

"I'm sorry it had to be done," said Colin, "and I'm sorry I killed the man, but I've been thinking about what you said in my shop earlier, and it made sense. Our businesses are at stake in this town—the well-being of our families. What kind of men would we be if we let a bunch of no-account bums ruin it for us? As you say, more lives would be lost in the long run if these fellows weren't put in their place today."

"I think you'll see little trouble from them, here on out," said Joe. "Didn't seem to be much fight left after Prescott was gone."

"I agree," answered Colin. "Besides, the town's all afire now with talk of electing a marshal. I don't think folks will put up with what has been going on in the past—not after what whey saw tonight. One thing Pablo and me would like to ask of you, though."

"What's that?" Corbett asked.

"Well, if you could see your way to stick around a few hours after daybreak, we sure could use another lesson with these shootin' irons."

CHAPTER 14

JOSÉ VALERO LOOKED out over the flat dry valley. Fifty miles to the north lay Trento's ranch. He remained for a moment, enjoying a fiery sunset glowing above the western slopes. Then he turned and walked back to camp.

"It's fine with me that we're not going to San Martin," he remarked. "The valley would be hell to cross."

"That's right," Joe said. He had built a small fire at a place where two giant stones lay together. Corbett was heating beans in a tin pan. "Besides, I'm hoping to stay clear of anyone who might spot us . . . until we can get up north and poke around a little. Keep to the high country, if you ask me."

"Agreed," said Corbett. "You don't want to have anything to do with that town. That would be trouble. We're headin' for your ranch, Joe. We need to check on your partner and your stock. Then you can go check out where that fellow was killed and I'll go into town. The main thing is to look out for your land and your property. That's my feeling anyhow."

Joe was edgy, but glad. They were back in his country now, and things would begin to happen. They were almost in sight of the mountains where his land was located. Still, questions gnawed at him . . . What had been happening to Al all this time? Did he have any stock left, or had it been rustled away? Would they get into a shooting war with the Milsteads?

As twilight settled over the plains and the men rolled into their blankets, Joe thought about the Milstead girls, especially Elizabeth. Too bad her family had become a foe, because it would have been nice to have a pretty young woman like her to court. Joe imagined the possibilities for a few minutes, before succumbing to exhaustion and the peaceful desert sounds.

As the men rode north the next morning, Joe was very much aware of how lush and verdant the land was in contrast to the barren hills and desert of the past week. These mountains were not all rock and scrub—there was plenty of green brush and tall pine. Grass grew in the open areas and small streams ran down from the higher elevations. Joe suddenly realized how desirable his ranch land must be, compared to most of the territory.

Corbett and Valero were also impressed. The young Mexican especially, unaccustomed to the more temperate north, marveled at the greenness around him. *"Mucha agua aquí,"* he commented after the group had crossed two streams in as many hours and had traveled half the day into increasingly attractive territory.

Joe and Corbett grinned, thinking of their boyhood homes back East. Valero, having grown up in the Chihuahuan desert, would be hard-pressed to imagine the lush, wet forests of Mississippi and Virginia.

"Mighty fine country you picked, Joey," Corbett said. "You'll do real well out here."

Joe swelled with pride.

Around midafternoon the men came to the rivulet that marked the eastern edge of Joe's land.

"Due west," said Joe, "there's a big valley with a stream along the eastern edge. Al and I have a shack by the stream there."

"Let's spread out," said Corbett. "If those Milsteads are poking around, we could ride right into 'em. José, you get about a quarter mile south, and I'll drift north a ways. When we get to the valley, stay in cover and just watch. I'll come by and fetch you both."

The men spread out and moved cautiously westward. Joe kept Blue on a forested ridge and let the horse take his time picking his way through stands of Douglas fir and white pine.

All was quiet. At one point there was a clear patch of hillside on Joe's right. He was familiar with the place. A fire had burned there years before; vegetation was now reclaiming the area, making for excellent forage. He had driven a dozen cows with calves to the clearing several weeks ago and was pleased to see them grazing there now. Perhaps the Milsteads hadn't helped themselves to his stock yet . . . or maybe they just hadn't discovered this bunch.

Before long, Joe found himself overlooking the valley he had just described to his companions. It was strange to see it again, after almost two weeks. There was the lean-to that he and Al Grundy had elaborated into a sort of shack. Nothing seemed disturbed. All was quiet.

Joe stayed back in the pines, watching. Blue stamped impatiently. Up the valley a ways grazed seven horses Joe recognized as his and Al's. Another good sign. Joe observed the shack again. No sign of Grundy . . . no fire . . . nothing.

Corbett approached, his sorrel gelding stepping softly on a carpet of pine needles. "No sign of anyone, far as I can tell," he said. "What about you?"

"Quiet," said Joe. "Maybe too quiet. I'd expect Al to be back in camp this time of day, were everything normal."

"Well, we can't speculate all day. Let's go down and have a look."

The two men walked their mounts south along the valley rim, looking for Valero.

Suddenly a shot rang out—then another. The two spurred their horses into a trot, the fastest gait possible among the trees and brush. Another shot, this from a different gun!

After a minute Joe and Corbett slowed to a walk and proceeded cautiously. An exchange of fire again. Joe peered through the trees and saw José Valero lying on the ground, aiming his rifle from behind a huge fir. His horse stood a dozen yards beyond. Joe signaled the Mexican with a low whistle. José looked over. He made a sweeping motion with his arm, signaling Joe and Corbett to circle around a small knoll, about a hundred yards off.

The two gunmen left their horses and began to move. No more shots had sounded and Trento began to wonder if their adversary had fled.

They stalked slowly, keeping to low-growing brush, finally coming up behind the hillock José had indicated. They stopped and peered.

Sitting comfortably against a large rock was a wiry, white-bearded man, his rifle also resting against the stone. The old fellow was chewing on a piece of jerky and swigging from a canteen. Occasionally, he craned his neck and stared down in the direction of José Valero. After one such inspection he casually reached for his firearm and levered off a shot in the direction of José. Joe and Thad glimpsed a darting movement as Valero ducked back behind his tree.

Joe grinned. He warned Corbett with a nudge, then shouted, "Listen here, old man! I brought you along to work, not picnic in the woods!"

The man jumped at the sound of Joe's voice. He swung the gun around, but saw no one.

"That you, Joe Trento? I'd know that voice anywheres! You come out now or I'll blast you, damn it!"

Joe laughed. "Hold on, old-timer, here we come!" The two walked forward.

"Damn you, Trento! Bad enough you go off fer days—who knows where—now you come sneakin' around, scarin' the hell out of me! J'ever consider callin' out?"

Joe and Corbett stood grinning. Joe said, "Sorry, Al—"

"And godammit! You've got that damn Thaddeus Corbett with you! You two been out having a good time together?" The old man was practically hopping up and down, but more out of excitement than anger. Joe began to speak, but was cut off again. "And who's that son of a bitch down there? Another one of your partners, I suppose?"

"That's right," said Joe, "and we've come back just to make sure you've got enough work to do. Looks like you've got some time on your hands though—"

"Damn you! Why, I oughta—"

"Hold on a minute," Corbett said. He stepped forward and called out in Spanish, then turned back. "Calm down, you two. Might be some of your Milstead buddies runnin' around these hills. How you been, Grundy? Been a long time."

"I'm gettin' along. Be a lot better, though, if I wasn't sneakin' around out here in the woods all week. Anybody mind tellin' me what in the hell's goin' on? I got me an idea, but let's hear it from you."

Valero came in, leading the horses. After an introduction, the four squatted down by Al's boulder and Joe related the events of the previous two weeks, beginning with being run down by the Milsteads and ending with the trip back through Maysville. Al Grundy listened quietly, except when Joe told about the expedition to get Deligro.

"Bastards," he said. "I'm up here running around like a rabbit, and you're down chasing outlaw Mexes."

"Sorry, old-timer," Joe said. "I'd have gotten word to you if I could've."

"Well, I picked up something of what was going on," said Grundy. "After you hadn't come back in two days, I rode on in to San Martin myself."

The others were interested. "What did you find?" Joe asked.

"Well, that tall young deputy, Billy Heywood, was there.

Said the marshal had been killed. Told me about the Milsteads bringin' you in on a murder charge, then you bustin' out. Said the whole town saw Spence Milstead shoot the marshal, but Spence rode out of town right quick and hasn't been seen.

"The other Milsteads stayed around, though. They was spreadin' word that the old marshal had been lettin' killers run free and escape from his jail . . . callin' him a coward . . . that sort of thing. They was pushin' for an election to be held for a new marshal—one to their liking, no doubt. They hung around a few days, drinkin' and carrying on, until old Billy called out Fergus Milstead. Milstead wouldn't come, but that put a damper on their spirits, and they eventually rode out.

"So I hightail it back here, and what do I find? Milsteads all over the place. They'd been through the shack and was headin' up the north slope, so I slipped back through the woods and came around on 'em. I put a few shots in the air and made 'em run, but they haven't gone far."

"So that's it," Joe said. "You're up here herding the Milsteads around."

"Yep," said the old man. "Been runnin' around ever since, peckin' away at those boys ever' once in a while . . . whenever I see 'em. I'm hopin' they think there's more'n just me up here."

"What about the stock? Been run off?"

"Some, maybe, but I been keepin' the Milsteads too nervous for them to do any real damage."

"Mighty peculiar," said Corbett. "Seems like they're waitin' for something. How many of them are there?"

"There's the old man," said Joe, "and Spence, if he's still around . . . then there's Fergus and Ev."

"And the Mexican kid," added Grundy. "And from what I've seen, a couple of drifters have thrown in with 'em. They might have six or seven guns."

"What d'you figure their plans are, Joey?" Corbett asked.

"I'd say they're simply trying to build a herd—from other folks' cattle, mostly—and let them scatter up in the high country. They'll prob'ly look for a market in a couple of years. Right now, I figure they're lookin' for me, or waitin' to see if I'll show. Al's kept them at bay for now, but eventually they'll get up the gumption to come on in."

"We're not in bad shape, then," said Corbett.

"How do you figure?"

"We've got 'em guessing. They'd like to have you out of the picture so they can run off your stock and have the range back, but they're too jumpy right now. That means they're not sure they can pull it off, and they're not sure about you. If they come up against some big trouble—like us—they'll most likely give up."

"That'd be fine," said Joe, "but I still have a murder charge to worry about. I'm itchin' to go look that spot over."

"And I still have a hankerin' to nose around town a bit," replied Corbett. "Joe, I vote the four of us stay down at your shanty tonight. It's a bold move—they'll certainly notice us—but that's the kind of message we want to send. Tomorrow you and I can ride out. José and Al can look out for each other."

Everyone was agreeable. They caught their mounts, stepped into the saddles, and headed for the big valley.

Joe was elated to be back. Riding into the expansive meadow, he felt the same excitement and pride as when he had arrived there months before.

The land was fine for ranching. Toward the north, the hills bunched rapidly into an impressive range, but here the terrain was rolling and lightly forested, with numerous sheltered valleys and canyons with good grazing. Corbett was right. It was best to get back on the land.

That evening, Joe and Al Grundy spent a few hours straightening up their place and taking stock of their possessions. It was obvious someone had gone through the place—objects were strewn about—but little if anything had been taken, perhaps because neither Joe nor Al had much of value, or perhaps because the vandals felt confident that they could return and plunder at a later time.

Corbett and José Valero took the opportunity to patrol the valley in the waning sunlight and further inspect Joe's holdings. The shack was at the foot of the eastern slope, so the two first rode west out into the clearing. Their horses trotted and cantered through lush grassland dotted with juniper and aspen. They splashed across a small stream and turned north. The grazing here would be as fine as any prairie land he'd ever seen, Corbett thought, although the landscape was different. The valley floor was rolling and varied, hiding numerous small ravines and dotted with much scrub and pine.

The land rose as the two continued north. They came upon and circled the grazing horses, which nickered in annoyance and trotted off.

Finally, the land rose steeply. Corbett spotted a trail that would allow horses and cattle to pass up into the higher land beyond, but he and Valero circled again and followed the perimeter of the valley back southward. Twice they saw the recent tracks of a half dozen horsemen entering or leaving the big meadow, but there was no other sign of intruders.

The two finally arrived back at the camp, remarking enthusiastically to Joe and Al about the beauty of the area.

They took turns that night standing watch: riding a ways up the hill in back of the shanty, then in a large sweep out into the valley. No trouble came.

In the morning, Corbett cleaned up and packed some provisions. He looked up as Joe walked in, leading Blue and the sorrel gelding.

"I'd feel better if two of you were going over there," Corbett said, "but I don't want to leave anyone alone here either."

"I'll slip in and out like a fox," Joe replied. "I'll likely be back for supper."

"You keep close to the trees, see what you want to see, then get out. You understand?"

"You're like an old hen nowadays, Thaddeus. You forgettin' that I snuck all the way to Mexico to find you?"

"That's what I mean. You're gettin' too big for your britches. These boys mean to kill you, Joey."

"I'll be careful," Joe said seriously. "Honest, Thad, all I want is a quick look. There may be something."

CHAPTER 15

THE TWO RODE out together, leaving José and the old man to tend to the camp and keep an eye on the valley.

Joe would cut straight across and head into the hill country to the west. He described the trail to San Martin to Corbett, and the two split up.

Joe rode to the edge of his property, where the hills grew steeper and the brush and forest became thicker. After a few miles of rough going, the land fell and the terrain opened up again, beginning the area claimed by the Milsteads. He had been depending on this ridge of tangled vegetation to keep his stock on his own land.

He descended the bluff into Milstead territory, trying to remember everything the family had revealed about the death of their hired hand. They had said Shorty had been working cattle not too far from their ranch house, close enough for the young girl, Millie, to ride out alone for a visit.

As Joe rode, it occurred to him that the land he was now seeing was not as good for beef as his own. This area was more heavily wooded, less open. So far he had not spotted much meadowland or other good grazing. That meant that there would be only a few spots within easy riding distance of the Milstead place where they could hold cattle.

Joe knew the approximate location of their cabins from comments heard around town. He headed in that direction.

Blue also seemed to be glad to be back in the high country. The gelding wove quietly and steadily through the stands of Douglas fir and piñon.

The ground finally became flat, and horse and rider emerged from the trees onto a small, open plain. Joe looked across and saw the Big Sandy river glimmering in the noonday sun. The flood plain stretched away to Joe's left and right, slipping out of sight as the river curved to the north. Several dozen head of beef grazed in that direction. Joe wondered whether this could be the spot.

Joe tapped his heels to Blue and moved on. He headed toward the cattle. He was fairly sure that the Milstead homestead lay to the south, and so he wanted to avoid that direction; at the same time, the land looked rougher to the north . . . and Joe had a hunch. The Milsteads might have lied about *where* Shorty died, just as they lied about Joe doing the killing.

Horse and rider traveled far enough out on the open ground to make the going easier, but close enough to the woods to remain inconspicuous. Joe now realized that the Big Sandy was just emerging from the mountains at this point, evolving from a tumbling mountain torrent into a more serene, smooth-flowing river. It would now take its time through these rolling hills, tracking south and west, eventually passing behind the town of San Martin.

As Joe had thought, the land ahead was more rugged. The river actually flowed out of a huge gorge, carving its path between stone walls covered with mossy vegetation. Joe passed the cattle, and the flood plain ended. He continued to parallel the river, moving up a wooded incline. He lost sight of the water, but could hear its sound. Arriving at the top of a hill, Joe followed the noise to his left, reining in abruptly after a minute. Horse and rider were perched at the edge of a precipice, the Big Sandy rushing along a hundred feet below.

Joe looked to the southwest. The view of hills, forest, and far-off desert was spectacular. The rushing water below, compared to the more placid river familiar to Joe, was likewise enthralling. He gazed down through the foam and spray and listened to the roar.

A checkered cloth caught his eyes. Blue and white, like a kerchief. Joe dismounted and squatted very close to the edge. He peered over. An arm . . . he could see an arm.

It was slow going, working his way along the rocky bank. Joe had to wade through the water at times, and the strong current nearly pulled his feet from under him. Finally he reached the body. The dead man was floating and bobbing in the rushing current, secured to the bank by a foot wedged between two roots. He was torn and mangled, and Joe could tell that he'd been dead for some time.

He was a smallish man, bearded and hairy, dressed more like a sodbuster than a stockman, and he had been shot in the back. Joe sloshed around for a better look. The dead man had no mustache, only a beard. It was definitely Shorty.

Another object caught Joe's eye. It was a large rucksack, stuck between some bushes a few feet above the water. Joe went to it and pulled it down. It was quite full. Joe removed a roll of blankets from the top and looked inside. First there was men's clothing—a number of shirts and several trousers. He pushed these aside and looked further. Dresses! Several rumpled and worn women's dresses were under the men's clothing. He pulled one out. It was rather small—just about the size of Millie Milstead. Along with the dresses there was a pair of girl's shoes and a small purse of some kind. It came to him in a flash—Millie hadn't just ridden out to visit Shorty that night, they had been eloping! Millie had given Shorty some of her things to put in his pack. But somehow they'd been caught and Shorty had been killed. No doubt the killer was one of the Milsteads, angry over the elopement, and the family had realized that they could use the situation to their advantage in order to frame Joe. Their mistake had been in claiming to have retrieved and buried Shorty's body themselves. They had made a point of it. They might not even know where the corpse had finally come to rest—but Joe did.

He looked at the pitiful remains of the murdered man. Not only had the Milsteads framed him, they had killed one of their own men to set the trap. Shorty and the marshal were dead, and the Milsteads were going to pay, Joe vowed to himself. He did what he could to ensure that the body remained in place in the chilled, rushing current, then turned away.

Joe caught Blue and stared back, but he continued on past the point where he had emerged onto the flood plain. At first he did not know why, then he realized he had an urge to see the Milstead place itself.

He was curious to find out more about these people. They were obviously a foul, dishonest, brutal lot, but they were also homesteaders who had brought female kin with them. Why had this family turned to thievery and murder?

Theirs was a pretty place for a spread, Joe thought as he rode at a walk along the edge of the trees, looking. Soon the cabins south of the meadow came into view. A pole corral was first, containing a half dozen horses and a pony. Next to this was a small stable. Beyond was another fence, separating the cabins from any wandering stock. The structures themselves looked nice enough—two modest log homes—not a lot of trash or busted equipment about, as was common to many frontier dwellings.

One building especially looked to have had a woman's touch. Curtains in the windows, even. Joe reined Blue into the woods a ways and dismounted. He stalked carefully through the trees, aiming for the point where the cabins were closest to the woods. He was being a fool, he knew, walking right into the lion's den, so to speak.

Joe stepped out of the evergreens and strode across a short space to the rear of the house. The single small window was set rather high up in the center of the wall, but Joe figured he was tall enough to peer in. He was correct. What he saw was the back room of the women's cabin, judging by the frills and accoutrements. A fancy comforter lay on a pole frame bed. Hairbrushes and a mirror rested on a wooden dressing table. A washbasin sat on its stand. A picture on the wall. More of a home than Joe Trento had seen in twelve years . . .

"Don't move an inch, mister, or I'll blast you!"

It was a female voice. Joe jerked his head around and looked into the eyes of Elizabeth Milstead.

"You!" she exclaimed. "But I thought you were miles from here!" She had a ten-gauge leveled at his belly.

Joe was not as worried about getting shot, or being discovered by the men, as he was embarrassed at being caught peeking into a young woman's bedroom!

"Sorry, Miss . . . ," Joe stammered, "I got a bit lost in the hills yonder . . . just tryin' to get my direction."

"By spying into our bedroom? If you're lost, why didn't you call out when you approached?"

"I suppose I wanted to see who lived here first. I'm awful sorry . . . I'll be on my way."

"You will not!" She snugged the gun up more tightly. "You're a wanted criminal. You broke right out of jail in San Martin and wounded two men on the way—and you killed our hand, Shorty!"

"Now, that isn't true, miss—"

"Marshal Parker apparently thought so, before . . ." She paused.

"Before your kin done him in," Joe snapped. "Use your head, Elizabeth. What do you really think these cousins of yours are up to? Back at the jail you yourself questioned whether Millie could have seen what she said she saw. Didn't her pa tell her what to say to the marshal?"

"I don't know . . ." The girl was startled by his outburst.

"Oh, yes you do! Maybe you can tell me where you all buried old Shorty? Give him a nice funeral, did you?"

"They said they buried him out in the hills."

"You get them to show you the place sometime. Your cousins are killers, Elizabeth, and I think you know it!"

"You better go . . . if you don't, I'll shoot and they'll come."

"I'll go. I meant you no harm, but you best do some thinking for yourself. Those boys have tried to steal my property and get me hung, and they've killed the marshal, as well as that poor hired hand out there. If you've had a part in all this, I hope you'll be able to sleep nights when it's over." Joe turned and walked away, still fuming.

Elizabeth Milstead lowered the shotgun. She bit her lower lip and watched Joe slip into the woods.

Despite his anger, Joe moved softly and silently through the brush. Finally his temper subsided. Poking around the dwellings had caused him to be caught by the girl, but at least he had found out that the men he had shot during his escape were not dead. He felt good about that.

And there was something about the girl's look by the time he had had his say . . . she seemed uncertain, and she'd let him leave. Maybe she would think about what he told her.

CHAPTER 16

JOE POINTED BLUE eastward, toward his own valley, and gave him his head. Finally they topped the tangled ridge and began to descend onto Joe's land. As they entered the big meadow, he spied a rider galloping flat-out toward him. He recognized Al's pinto and waited, wondering.

"On my way to look for you," Grundy said as he slid to a stop. "Them cayuses are back, and this time it's trouble."

"What's up?" asked Joe.

"Don't know fer sure. José was out scoutin' this mornin' and spotted the bastards ridin' across the place. Six of 'em. That's more'n I've seen together at one time. He fetched me up and we followed 'em to the burnt place where we left those cows."

The two had started off at a trot as Grundy spoke. "You think they knew about the cows?" Joe asked.

Grundy nodded. "I figger they stumbled on 'em before and saw that they was easy pickin's, all bunched up like that, and with calves. The sonsabitches are too lazy to round up the stock we've got up north."

"Where's José now?"

"He's out there, watchin' 'em. If they start to move out with the stock, he'll do what he can to hold 'em, but he's waitin' fer us."

"If they get those cows and calves onto their land," said Joe, "we'll have a helluva time gettin' 'em back."

They stopped at the shanty long enough to grab some extra cartridges, then rode out. Within a half hour they were close enough to the burn to dismount and proceed on foot. They neared the spot where José Valero lay hidden. Joe whistled softly.

"They spent a while sitting and smoking," reported José, "before they got to work."

"Good," said Joe. "Three guns will be a lot better than one."

Joe crawled forward through the brush until he could peer down the hillside. It was the Milsteads, all right. They were all there except the old man, Cal. Joe recognized Ev, Fergus, Chico, and even Spence, as well as two cowboys he had never seen before.

Joe observed that the Milsteads knew something about driving stock. They had bunched the herd up in one end of the clearing without exciting or upsetting the animals, which continued to graze calmly. The men sat on horseback, probably discussing the details of their trail home.

It wouldn't be easy to drive stock across the forested and hilly terrain, but if they kept the cattle calm and moving slowly, it could be done. Joe returned to the others.

"Well, we can't let 'em get away. Let's get in front of 'em. When they start to move out, we'll open up. Don't shoot to kill right off . . . let's see if they'll run."

The trio positioned themselves in the trees just west of the clearing. The Milsteads finally made up their minds and started to move. Instead of the usual cracking of whips and loud whoops, however, the men slowly and quietly pushed the herd into the forest.

When most of the cows were into the trees, Joe decided it was time. He spotted Spence Milstead's profile through a tangle of limbs, aimed his Winchester high, and fired. José and Al opened up as well, and within an instant they had put a dozen bullets in the air.

The Milsteads, taken completely by surprise, required a few moments to bring their mounts under control and draw their weapons. They suffered from the disadvantage of remaining in the open while their opponents were hidden.

Joe and his companions had spread themselves apart among the trees and brush, dashing from time to time from behind cover to new positions in the forest. These tactics confused the rustlers as to the number and exact location of their adversaries.

Several of the Milstead group drew pistols and fired into the trees. A few of the others tried to retrieve the cattle, which were bolting wildly, but it soon became obvious that their position was hopeless.

"Give 'em up!" Spence finally shouted, indicating the frightened cattle. "Head uphill and dismount!" He pulled his buckskin around and lunged up the hillside, followed by the others.

"Damn!" Joe muttered. Spence was smarter than he'd thought. The band was heading to higher ground, which would provide them a slight advantage. Also, instead of running as Joe had hoped, the rustlers apparently intended to fight back.

The firing ceased momentarily. Joe knew that he needed a plan badly . . . and quickly. They were outnumbered two to one.

Joe thought back to what he knew of this kind of fighting from the war. The Rebs were always full of tricks to make up for being outnumbered and outgunned.

Joe took advantage of the temporary lull in order to slip from tree to tree, signaling to his companions to join him. The three squatted together in a gully while Joe whispered a plan. In a moment they were each crawling off and spreading out.

A rifle shot split the afternoon silence, coming from the direction of the rustlers. José and Al returned fire and the fight was on again. Joe and his friends held their ground for several minutes, then began to move. Each one in turn bolted from his cover and fell back several yards to a new spot. The Milstead band noticed the activity and, encouraged by the retreat, moved forward with renewed enthusiasm.

Joe and his friends maneuvered themselves to within a few yards of their mounts, which remained out of sight in a ravine. Their adversaries, more encouraged than ever, marched over the rough terrain in pursuit.

"Run for it!" Joe shouted suddenly, loud enough for all to hear. The three men disappeared over the side of the ravine, but reappeared seconds later, mounted, lashing the horses into a mad gallop westward.

"After 'em!" shouted Spence Milstead. "Let's finish the bastards once and for all!" The Milsteads turned and ran for their own mounts, and in a moment were galloping in pursuit and whooping with excitement.

Spence and Fergus led the pack. Soon they were able to spy one of the fleeing men through the trees. It was Valero, loping his pony rather easily, allowing the pursuers to gain some ground. Joe and Grundy were nowhere in sight. Fergus let out a war cry and fired off a wild shot. Valero turned and eyed his enemies. Then he tapped his heels to his wiry cayuse and took off like a shot.

"Goddamnit, they're gettin' away!" cried Spence. All the men spurred their mounts and rushed headlong through leaves and limbs, fearful of losing their quarry.

A shot sounded on their left flank, and the Milsteads saw one of their own fly from the saddle, a spray of blood in the air. A volley of shots followed, seemingly from all directions. Ev Milstead jerked forward and toppled from the saddle. Once again the group pulled up in confusion.

"They've doubled back!" yelled Spence. More shots out of nowhere, and someone screamed in pain. "Bastards have us surrounded," called Spence, now worried himself. His group milled about a moment longer—a few fired sporadically up and down the mountainside—while Joe

and his friends kept a continual whistle of bullets in the
air around their heads.

Spence saw his brother Ev rise from the ground, bleeding. "Let's get out of here, boys . . . head for home!" He
reached down and hauled Everett up behind him, then
trotted over and grabbed his brother's horse.

None of the others hesitated after hearing Spence's
order. Each spurred his mount and bolted off through
the trees. Two of the men passed within inches of where
Joe lay hidden in a dense thicket.

The mountainside grew strangely still as the hoofbeats
faded into distant silence. Joe and the others remained
quiet for several minutes until they were certain that the
gang had gone. Joe emerged and walked forward; José
and Al followed.

They came to the dead man, shot through the chest by
Valero. "He saw the sun reflect off of my rifle," said José.
"I had to kill him—he was about to shout to the others."

"It's a good thing," said Joe. "These boys have been tryin'
to do me in all along. They'd have killed us if they'd gotten
the chance."

"Could've killed each goddamn one of 'em if we'd a
wanted," said Grundy, "and I'll bet they know it, too." He
bent over and peered closely at the dead man. "I'll be
damned! This here's Jade Cutler! Haven't seen 'im in a
coupla years, but it's him, all right. I recollect that scar."

Joe had heard the name many times. Jade Cutler was
one of his kind in a way—a gunfighter and former trail
hand—but he had turned killer. Not like Corbett or himself, who had also killed, but a true killer, who worked
virtually as an assassin.

"Just the type to buddy up to Spence Milstead," Al
remarked. "They probably made him a few promises so
he'd throw in."

"Well, we're lucky he's out of the way," Joe said. "These
Milsteads aren't backing down, from the looks of it. After

this, that Spence'll be madder than ever, and he'll be lookin' for another fight. We need to get hold of Thaddeus."

They took the dead man's gun and ammunition—not out of greed, but rather due to a frugality common to most frontier folk, who could not see the sense in letting good equipment be ruined or wasted.

Cutler's mount had followed the Milstead horses back westward. Joe and José scraped a shallow grave for the body and then gathered stones to place on top. They finished their work and turned their backs on the grave with scarcely another thought. The death of a gunman was a common occurrence.

After a short stop to see that the cows and calves were again grazing peacefully, the three men returned to camp. Joe and Al discussed the possibility of one of them heading into San Martin to look for Corbett, but they decided against it. After all, he had been gone only one day and would likely require more time than that in order to do his scouting. Also, without knowing when or how the Milsteads might strike again, it behooved them to all remain on the place to stand guard.

As evening came on, the three fell into their routine of patrolling the valley and surrounding hillsides or working around the camp. They took turns standing guard that evening, and the next morning Joe and Valero even began staking out and digging postholes for corrals and a barn. These were things that a working ranch needed, and Joe was anxious to get them under construction.

A real house, also, was often on his mind. He had lived in the open for so long that permanent walls and a roof almost seemed unnecessary. Perhaps it was the years without a home that made him desire one even more . . . at any rate, the winters here would be colder than in Texas, so a ranch house would be needed.

The afternoon slipped by uneventfully. As he had several times over the past week, Joe found himself in an oddly tranquil mood, given the turmoil of the situation. It must be the country, he thought. To be constantly under the open sky, roaming widely through wild, sparsely peopled land had a certain effect on a man.

Valero had returned to the shack to help prepare a meal. Joe stood in the field, leaning on his shovel, enjoying the view and his thoughts.

He spotted the rider several minutes before he could hear the hoofbeats. A girl was galloping toward him, her golden brown hair reflecting in the lowering sun.

CHAPTER 17

FELIPE DELIGRO WAS uncomfortable and irritable, standing in the hot sun.

Damn that Raul! What was taking him so long? When the two had arrived in San Martin, Raul had been clever enough to find employment sweeping out the saloon every morning in exchange for a cup of coffee and some beans. He had told the owner that they had come far to the north, looking for work, and were staying with a cousin for a few weeks before heading back to Mexico.

Deligro removed his sombrero and mopped his wet forehead with a rag. He reminded himself that he was here on business . . . that this was for Carlos, his brother. Raul's real purpose was to gather information on the men who had captured Carlos and wiped out half of the gang.

He himself had been able to slip away into the nearly impassable badlands south of the border. Some of the others had done likewise. Deligro had tried to rally them to regroup in one of their old hiding places, but they would have none of it. It had been a terrible defeat, and many had died, and without the forceful leadership of Carlos, who had been hanged by the citizens of Morelos, morale had plummeted. Most of the cutthroats had drifted back to their peasant lifestyles in the towns and countryside of the region.

That had angered Deligro immensely. Was there not one man with enough *huevos* to help avenge his brother's death? Well, he would show them what a real man could do. When the word spread that he personally had killed the famous Thaddeus Corbett, the men would think again.

Not only would Carlos be avenged, but a major threat to the gang's operations would be gone.

The huge Mexican's eyes caught sight of the deputy stepping out of his office. At first he had been glad to find out that this young gringo was the only law left in San Martin after the marshal had been killed—but soon it had become apparent that there was much tension in the little town. A group of Anglos was stirring up trouble—a tough-looking bunch. Exactly what was going on, he did not know, but Felipe worried about it.

The deputy crossed the street and entered the saloon. He wouldn't find much at this hour, Deligro thought. If the pattern of the past few days held true, the belligerent gang of gringos would arrive midafternoon to begin their carousing. The tall deputy always had some sort of confrontation with them . . . except for yesterday. For some reason, the gang did not show up yesterday.

Deligro cursed Raul, who was probably loitering in the coolness of the saloon while he stood sweating in the sun!

He was *un buen amigo,* however. After Deligro had made his way back to a whore's shack on the outskirts of Morelos, Raul had sought him out. Raul had also melted away after the battle, but he'd returned to the town, where he had relatives, then came looking for Deligro. He was the only loyal one out of them all.

The deputy exited the saloon, strode down the walk, and entered the dry-goods store.

It had been Raul, snooping around Morelos, as was his custom, who had first learned that the gringos had been purposely sent to wipe out the gang. He also learned about the man who headed the effort—Corbett. This too angered Deligro. Of course the merchants and ranchers would fight the bandits—after all, they were protecting their businesses and property. This was understandable. But Corbett—the gang was no threat to him! He was a hired soldier, willing to kill for pay.

Raul's snooping had also revealed that Corbett was planning a trip north with two companions who had also been part of the posse. Their destination was the town called San Martin. Deligro and Raul had set off immediately themselves for San Martin.

"You! Mexican!" shouted a deep voice. Deligro whirled around with surprising quickness. There stood a grinning Raul.

"Goddamnit, you weasel! You are lucky I have no guns. I would kill you." The two had shed their weapons and donned peasant garb before entering town.

"*Tranquilo, hombre,*" said Raul, returning to his own voice. "We still need to have some fun, no?"

"It will be fun for me to see that dirty gringo die, that is all. What have you found out?"

"It is him. He came in very early for coffee, then rode out of town, returning about half an hour ago. He uses another name, a Mister Nilsson, I think. Says he is here to buy land."

"What about the others?"

"Nothing. Corbett is here alone, staying at the hotel."

"We should have followed them here, instead of riding ahead."

"Yes, then we would know more."

Deligro rubbed his unshaven chin and eyed the main street of San Martin. "I don't like it," he said. "I don't want to try anything unless I know where those other bastards are."

"I think he waits for them," suggested Raul. "He spends a lot of time sitting and looking around. Maybe they're going to pull a job."

Could be, thought Deligro. He didn't know which side of the law Corbett preferred. He could be casing the town for a holdup. Maybe Corbett had something to do with those other gringo troublemakers. Deligro and Raul could find themselves gravely outnumbered if they were not careful.

"*Vamanos*," he said, stepping into the street. "We go get some dinner. We can check on this gringo later."

Thad Corbett sat on the bed in his hotel room and rolled a cigarette. It was the afternoon of his second day in town, and so far he had made a good show of being a rancher from Texas scouting new range, but he'd not seen nor heard as much as he'd expected. He had, however, picked up a little information from various conversations. Corbett lit up and lay back on the bed, blowing smoke at the ceiling and reviewing what he knew.

Apparently the town was very upset over a series of tragic events. First, a killer had been brought in, accused of rustling and killing a local cowhand. Next, the marshal was cut down by Spence Milstead, whose family most of the townsfolk were afraid of anyway. Then the young stranger escaped from jail amid a hail of gunfire during which more men were shot. Ever since, the town had been filled with drunkenness and fighting and flaring tempers.

Deputy Marshal Billy Heywood had returned to town on the evening of his boss's death to be immediately challenged himself. He no longer had a prisoner to worry about, but he himself would be fired and run out of town if the Milstead gang had its way.

Many of the townsfolk were so weary and fearful of the fighting and gunplay that they supported Spence and Ev Milstead's daily calls for a new marshal. Perhaps an older, stronger lawman could bring some calm to the town. The Milsteads proposed Jade Cutler, an acquaintance who they claimed was an ex-lawman. He would bring a strong arm and stern law to San Martin, they said.

For his part, Billy Heywood had announced that he was still the law in San Martin, and nothing would change until a federal marshal arrived to investigate Josh Parker's death. Billy was supported by the majority, if not the most vocal, of the citizenry. He continued to occupy the jail-house and make his usual routine patrols of the town, only now he went armed with a double-barreled shotgun in addition to his six-shooters.

Spence had disappeared after the shooting of Parker. Billy had demanded that his brothers tell Spence to give himself up, but of course he did not appear.

The deputy had heard nothing so far from the federal marshal, although several telegraphs had been sent. His hope was that one or more territorial officials would show up to help suppress the hot tempers and put together a posse to go after Spence. He would have liked to go after Spence himself, but didn't dare leave the town lawless under the current circumstances.

Billy had mixed feelings concerning Joe Trento. He told people he thought Trento was innocent but he belonged back in jail until cleared of the murder charge.

Each night as he made his rounds the deputy was inevitably stopped by Fergus, Everett, and some of their buddies. They would demand that he step down and call for an election; Billy would ignore their insults and warn the group to tone down their disturbances and get out of his way. He was only one man, but none of the cowardly gang had enough nerve to push him very far. They knew that he carried the scattergun for a purpose, and that he knew how to use it.

Corbett sat up and crushed out his smoke on the wooden floor. He strolled over to the window and stared down into the street. For some reason, the Milstead outfit had skipped coming to town yesterday, breaking what was apparently their usual pattern . . .

It might be best to wait things out. If federal authorities did arrive, they might put a few of Joe's adversaries behind bars and even clear Joe of the murder charge. They could handle things up at the ranch afterward, in their own style.

Six riders appeared from the north and trotted down Main Street. Corbett watched as they reined up and dismounted in front of the Red Dawn saloon. It looked like the Milsteads, judging by Joe's descriptions—dirty, tough-looking men, well-worn gear, and tied-down side arms. Only the old man was missing—had he overheard something about that?—and of course, Spence was hiding out.

Tough looking but not tough acting . . . at least not right now. Corbett had expected a swaggering, boisterous bunch; this group looked serious but subdued.

The group disappeared through swinging doors and suddenly Thad Corbett felt like having a beer.

Elizabeth Milstead's chestnut pony slid to a stop and stood gasping for breath. "I thought you might be gone—out with your stock. I'm glad you're here."

She was breathing hard, too. Joe stepped forward to help her down.

"Are you all right? You've about run this pony to death. Something happen at your place?"

"The boys rode back in last night . . . told me about the fight. You killed Cutler. I'm glad—Lord forgive me—because he was an evil man, but it's put them in an ugly mood. They were depending on him."

"I'm not sure I understand."

"Who can understand my family? As you have probably guessed, they'd planned to make their fortunes running cattle on the range north of the San Martin valley. When you came along, you took a chunk of what they'd planned to use, including this very valley. That meant that they would have to run a legitimate, organized outfit in order to make a go of it on just their own land, and they're not up to that."

José Valero rode up. "Trouble, *amigo*?"

"Don't know yet," said Joe. He turned to the girl. "I know they want to run me off—that's obvious—but I've no intention of leaving. You can tell them so."

"No, I can't," she replied. "I don't plan to ever see them again."

"Why not?"

"Millie and I will be gone when they get back."

"Back from where?"

"That's what I rode out to tell you. They've gone to town, and I believe they're going to murder Billy Heywood. They've been justifying Josh Parker's death by saying that he was weak—that he permitted killing and allowed you to escape.

"The townsfolk are afraid of the wild goings-on in the area. With Parker dead, some would like to elect a tough new marshal. The boys were going to push for Jade Cutler. Now I think they'll try to elect Fergus or even Spence."

Spence Milstead . . . a lawman! "You reckon folks'd go for that?"

"No, but there's a possibility it might get pushed through."

"Why are you telling us this, Elizabeth?"

"I found Shorty's body. After you left yesterday I went looking. Then I had a talk with Millie and found out the truth. I'd had the feeling that something was wrong from the start, but I didn't want to believe it. I came out here hoping for a new life—in a good place, where people can raise families and make a good living." She paused briefly, looking off across the grassland. "After seeing Shorty, then learning of the boys' plans, I couldn't bear it anymore."

"So you're going to leave?"

"Yes. I won't be part of any more killing. I'll take Millie and go back East to relatives. The boys will more than likely be glad to be rid of us."

"What about the old man?" Joe asked.

"Uncle Cal? I don't know. He's as bad as the rest of them. He's gone looking for you, you know."

"What?"

"He hired a gunman who had ridden in with Cutler. Billy Heywood had picked up your trail circling around town and heading south, but had not followed far. Uncle Cal knew about it and decided to go after you himself. Said he'd bring you in if Heywood couldn't."

Crazy old buzzard, Joe thought. "When did your cousins leave for town?"

"Around midmorning."

Joe shot a glance at Valero, who suddenly looked worried.

"I'm sorry," she said. "I should have come right away, but I couldn't decide."

The three made their way back to the shack, where they told Al the news.

"If what you say is true," Grundy said, "that deputy could be dead already. I doubt they'll even give 'im a fighting chance. No offense, ma'am."

"I bet Thad will step in if he's still there," said Joe. "That might help."

"Might get 'em both killed," replied Al. "Even two guns against six or seven ain't good odds."

Joe looked across his land to the west. The sun was a huge orange ball, just beginning its descent behind the mountains. "Still about an hour of daylight left," he muttered to himself. He turned to the girl. "Are you sure the whole gang rode into town? You sure none headed over to raid my place again?"

"I saw them heading out of sight toward San Martin," said Elizabeth. "They had it all planned out. I'm sure they all went together."

Joe turned back to his companions. "Boys, I figure this thing may not get out of hand until around midnight. If we ride now, we can be there by then. That'd even up the odds some."

"Then let's saddle up," said Grundy.

Valero and Grundy headed off to get ready, and Joe turned to the girl. "At the north end of my valley there's a trail leading up to a canyon in the hills. I've got stock farther out, but about a hundred yards up there's an arroyo that cuts off from the main canyon. There's an abandoned prospector's cabin there. It's old but sturdy. I want you to get Millie and go there."

"What for?" asked the girl.

"No one knows about the place," explained Joe. "The trail's hidden by brush. You'll be safe there should things go wrong somehow."

"I've already told you, we're going east. Thank you, but we'll get along just fine."

"Elizabeth, use your head . . . two girls traveling alone through this country? There are still plenty of Apaches about."

"Nonsense. Millie and I ride for miles through these hills almost every day. Stop treating us like children."

Joe was at a loss for words and his feelings were confused. She was right—he could not tell her what to do. She was not his woman, or his kin. The young man knew that he had more and better reasons for wanting the girl to stay, but he could not find the words.

Valero cantered in, driving three fresh horses in front of him. Grundy emerged from the lean-to, lugging saddlebags and rifles. Joe stared off to the west.

"Can't blame you, I reckon, if you head back East. This is a rough country, and you've surely had a rough time of it. But what you said before . . . about wanting a decent place for people . . . and families . . . well, I reckon a lot of us feel that way. If you leave now, it'll be like giving up. But if you stayed on—"

"Joe, let's move," cut in Al. "The more daylight we have, the faster we can travel."

José led Blue up, and Joe took the reins. He addressed the girl. "Will you be all right? I mean, getting back to your place?"

"I'll be fine," she replied, but not defensively now.

The men mounted up. Joe looked at Elizabeth. He wanted to say more, but felt embarrassed. He started to turn away, then she spoke.

"About a hundred yards north?" she asked.

Joe stared for a moment. "That's right. Hidden by the brush." He pulled his horse around and cantered off toward the orange ball in the sky.

CHAPTER 18

FEDERAL MARSHAL JACK Keyes glanced up as someone else entered the Red Dawn saloon. He gave the new man a quick look. He guessed this was not the deputy, Billy Heywood. Neither did the man appear to be an aquaintance of the dirty-looking bunch that had arrived ten minutes earlier—no "howdys" or nods of recognition. Didn't look much like a businessman, or even a local rancher. Something about him though . . . subtle differences in the clothes, the walk . . . something about the type of holster, the way it was worn.

The newcomer stepped up next to Jack Keyes without a glance and ordered a beer.

The marshal had told the bartender he was just passing through—a Texas boy returning home from California. Jack Keyes had slipped into town quietly, left his horse at the livery and his badge in his pocket. He'd walked down the street to the Red Dawn and had tried to remain inconspicuous.

He'd come in response to a telegram. San Martin was in the middle of some kind of battle over grazing range. Such conflicts were common: One man shoots another, perhaps justifiably, perhaps not. One group tries to buy or somehow gain influence over the local law. But this time the town marshal had been murdered, and that made the range war a more serious matter.

Keyes had checked on the names in the telegram. Joe Trento had legal title to land in the county, adjoining land still in the public domain. Concerning the other group, the Milsteads, he'd found nothing.

He had seen enough of range disputes to know that nothing was ever cut-and-dried. Both sides may have killed, both sides may have legitimate gripes. The only way an outsider could get to the bottom of it all was to come in quietly and look . . . listen.

Keyes had no idea that the man standing next to him was gathering information too, only for different reasons.

Outside, a huge Mexican sat on a shady bench. He had nodded good-naturedly to both the marshal and Corbett as each had passed. As the afternoon grew to a close, Deligro finally heaved himself up and walked off. He had come to a decision.

A few minutes later, Keyes finished his drink and left the saloon. He had discovered very little from the comments he had overheard. The saloon seemed somehow slow, subdued. He decided to go to the hotel and get a room and a meal. He'd return to the Red Dawn later, after everyone was drunk.

At a table away from the bar, Ev and Fergus Milstead talked in low voices. Chico and another man sat quietly and listened. The plan was for Spence to show up later in the evening and remain in the shadows outside. They'd wait for the deputy to make his rounds. It wouldn't be a fancy showdown. Their move would be sudden and deadly.

Billy Heywood stood in the doorway of the dry-goods store and watched a big Mexican he did not recognize move down the street. Nothing unusual about him, but Billy had an odd feeling about the stranger.

The strain of the last few weeks had made his features tense and haggard. Billy Heywood knew that most of the citizens of San Martin supported him and wanted him to stay on as their lawman. Many had given him quick words of encouragement, in passing, when none of the Milstead cronies were within earshot. Yet, Heywood also knew that most of the townsfolk were not gunmen. They were home-steaders, tradesmen, sodbusters. The Milsteads knew this, too. It was only a matter of time before they screwed up the courage to challenge him for control of the town.

They might think of him as a young, green deputy, but he was faster than most people knew. He had killed before, and he was tough. If it came to fighting, they would see just how tough he was. He hoped, however, that the federal officers he had telegrammed would show up first.

Tough also were the three riders heading toward town from the north. Each had fought battles before and knew what to expect, so they rode quickly and quietly, each with his own thoughts.

Joe tried to think of a plan. José and Al would be looking to him to lead off when it was time. He was the fastest, he knew who to kill first, and he would not hesitate.

Joe was tense, but glad. Tonight would be the end of it. Either they would put a big enough hole in the Milstead gang to break their hold on the San Martin valley, or they themselves would be run off—maybe killed.

They would reach the town late in the evening, perhaps close to midnight. The Milstead boys, at best, would be planning a standoff and shoot-out with Billy. At worst, they would ambush him somewhere in the dark. Either method amounted to murder, and the deputy stood little chance.

Joe decided it would be best for the three of them to split up before reaching town. If the three of them rode down Main Street, the Milsteads would take it as a challenge and go to shooting right off. It would be better to come in separately. Joe instructed José and Grundy to lay low, blend in with any Saturday-night strollers, look for Thad, and watch for trouble. Hopefully, they'd be able to spot the Milsteads' play in time to put some lead in the air first . . . if they weren't too late.

They rode through the cool night air. Stars spread out overhead like a huge glittering blanket. The men ate away at the miles, alternately walking, trotting, and cantering their mounts southward.

Finally they stopped. The desert was quiet except for the heavy breathing of the animals. A mile or so ahead, twinkling in the black night, was San Martin. The three trotted off in different directions.

The Red Dawn saloon had become increasingly lively. As the evening progressed, more cowboys and cardplayers had wandered in, music had begun, and much beer and whiskey had been poured. Even the sullen-looking Milsteads began to laugh and call out as their gambling and drinking partners filtered in.

Occasionally, Chico would slip out and return five or ten minutes later. Twice he returned and gave a short shake of his head. About ten o'clock, however, he rushed into the saloon, pushed through the crowd, and whispered to Fergus that Spence had arrived. Fergus told Everett. The two turned instantly more jovial. They yelled to their companions and ordered a fresh round of whiskeys.

Across the street, in the darkness behind the jailhouse, crouched Spence Milstead, chuckling inwardly. That beanpole deputy would love to bring him in—at least that's what he'd been saying around town. Well, he'd be right over his head tonight, and the lawman wouldn't even know it! A pretty clever idea, he thought. He leapt up and softly grasped the edge of the jailhouse roof. Like a giant, hairy cat, he pulled himself up and threw a leg onto the roof. In a moment, he was stepping quietly up to the peak and peering down at the street.

Spence knew, as did everyone familiar with San Martin, that the deputy would make his rounds every hour on a Saturday night, until all was quiet. Lately, of course, these rounds were interrupted by the jeering and complaining of his brothers, who would spill out of the saloon and onto the walk as Heywood went by. Tonight Fergus would confront the deputy face-to-face and insist that he give up his badge. Billy would refuse. Fergus would go for his gun, but Spence, up there on the roof, would have a bead on the deputy and would squeeze the trigger as soon as Heywood made a move.

Finally, he thought, we can put an end to this business. They may have gotten Cutler, but that wouldn't matter much. With Ev or Fergus in as marshal, things would finally start going their way . . . here in town as well as out on the range.

Joe Trento squatted in the darkness of a Main Street alley. It was several buildings down from the jailhouse and almost directly across from the Red Dawn. He could hear the typical jovial laughter and clinking of glassware coming from the saloon. All seemed normal in town so far. Somewhere across the street José Valero was also hiding. Grundy was positioned at the edge of town, up by the livery.

Joe wondered about Thad Corbett. This had been Corbett's second day in town, and for all Joe knew, Corbett had found what he'd come to find and had already left. It didn't matter, though—they'd still stay to help Heywood.

He continued to peer at the crowd visible beyond the saloon's bat-wing doors, trying to identify the faces. Once, he saw Everett, arm in a sling—too bad it was only his left arm. There was still no sign of Corbett.

Joe assumed that the deputy was in the jailhouse. The Milsteads and their crowd were obviously in the saloon. Joe counted ten ponies hitched outside of the Red Dawn.

Not much more to do but sit and wait, thought Joe. When Heywood gets called out, it will be up to Valero, Grundy, and him to look for and find the hidden guns, for undoubtedly there would be at least one. They would do what they could when the time came.

Joe reckoned it was about ten-thirty when the jailhouse door opened and then swung shut with a thud. He crouched in the shadows and watched. He heard footsteps fading away. Heywood must have emerged to make his rounds. Joe wished he could look down the street, but did not dare leave the alley. Others, he suspected, besides himself and his companions, were watching through the darkness.

He grew impatient and a little nervous. Finally after about ten minutes, he saw a figure walking back his way, only on the opposite side of the street. He recognized Billy Heywood. A man wearing an apron emerged from a small shop.

"Evenin', Deputy." Joe heard him faintly. The man said more but Joe couldn't make it out.

" 'Bout that time of year," Heywood replied. The deputy and shopkeeper looked up at the clear, crisp sky for a moment. They bid each other goodnight, and parted. Heywood moved toward the Red Dawn.

Joe tensed. This could be it. He hoped Valero and Grundy were watching. Billy Heywood entered the saloon.

He's got guts, Joe thought. A lot of deputies, marshals too, would hide in their jailhouse.

The volume of noise coming from the saloon fell to a murmur. Joe heard Heywood's voice saying something. Another voice after that. The talk and laughter slowly returned to normal, and Joe let out a deep sigh. Heywood left the saloon and continued his patrol. Someone from inside shouted something and everyone laughed.

Heywood crossed the street at the far end of town and headed back toward Joe. Joe shrank further back into the shadows as the deputy crossed in front of him. He heard the lawman stomp back into the jailhouse.

Nothing to do but wait some more. The hotel was on

Joe's side of the street, too, and occasionally he heard voices coming from its front porch. Shortly after Billy had finished his rounds, a man stepped off the hotel porch and crossed the street to the Red Dawn. Joe peered through the night, hoping to recognize the features of Thad Corbett. No, too short. A short, slim man, middle-aged, dressed like a cowboy, but neat looking. Probably a visitor to town.

Time passed and nothing happened. Joe Trento's concentration wandered. He thought of his ranch . . . the events of the past week . . . Pablo down in Maysville . . . the girl who might be waiting in the canyon.

Joe's attention was drawn to the increasing noise over at the Red Dawn. As the night had passed, the patrons had grown drunker and louder. Some had spilled out onto the sidewalk to do their loafing in the cool night air. Inside, the crowd occasionally quieted while someone made a short speech.

More exited the saloon. Some even stood talking in the street. It was about time for Heywood to make his rounds again. Ordinarily, a marshal might come around and herd these fellows back into the saloon—maybe even break them up for the night. Not this bunch, though. Joe did not envy anyone the job of clearing the sidewalk tonight.

For a moment, he thought they should change their strategy. Maybe Grundy and Valero belonged inside the saloon, where they could speak up and stand with Billy when the time came. That might have worked if they'd thought of it, but not now.

Sure enough, Joe soon heard the familiar bang of the jailhouse door. To his surprise, he saw that the deputy did not head down the walk as was his custom, but instead moved straight across the street to the saloon. He approached a group of men.

"You boys about ready to head out?" he asked. One man replied and the others laughed. Joe could not make out the words. Heywood said a few words more, then passed through into the Red Dawn.

Damn, thought Joe. He didn't want the deputy out of his sight. He wanted the action to take place in the street. He stepped out of the alley and stood in the shadows in front of a small shop. The saloon was across the street and several buildings north. Joe tried to hear what was going on inside of it; instead he heard a shuffling sound coming from his side of the street—somewhere nearby. It wouldn't be Grundy or Valero. Corbett, maybe?

Suddenly, Billy Heywood exited the saloon and headed down the street, threading his way through the men standing outside. A second later the bat-wing doors banged open again and Fergus and Everett Milstead bolted through, followed by some others.

"Heywood!" shouted Fergus Milstead, bounding into the street. The young deputy turned and faced the crowd. "We want you out! You've been puttin' us off too long. You either ride out of town tonight, or we run you out!"

"You're a fool, Milstead!" replied Heywood. "I'm not goin' anywhere and you know it. When the federal marshal gets here, he'll decide what happens in San Martin. Until then, I'm the law here!"

This was it. Joe scanned the crowd, trying to figure how the thing would develop. Then he heard the noise again. Someone else was close by.

CHAPTER 19

"DAMN THE FEDERAL marshal!" cried Everett. "He may not get here for weeks—months, maybe. The people of this town want their own lawman now!"

"Forget it, Ev!" said Heywood. "You men get back inside to your beer or head on home—I don't care which—unless you want to spend the night behind bars!"

"The hell we will!" shouted Fergus.

"That's enough!" someone called. It was the slim, neat-looking man Joe had seen before. He stepped through the saloon doors. "I'm Jack Keyes, United States marshal."

Fergus shot him a glance, then looked back to Heywood. He growled in rage—and went for his gun.

As Joe started his draw he heard the scuffling sound again—this time louder. On a hunch, he dove and spun, looking behind and up. There was Spence Milstead, aiming a rifle from the rooftop!

Joe knew he'd be too late. As he vainly raised his Colt toward the rooftop, Valero's .45 fired behind him, and Spence Milstead jerked and fell backward, his own weapon firing harmlessly skyward as shots erupted in the street.

Joe turned and dove behind a wagon. Looking out from behind spoked wheels, Joe saw a main street filled with hellfire. A waxing moon had risen, casting a soft light on the violent scene. Another series of shots sounded, and muzzle blasts momentarily illuminated the storefronts. Joe took in what he could in that instant.

Fergus Milstead lay dead in the street, bloodied by more than one bullet. Everett and some others had taken cover behind a trough and some barrels, having been pushed back some distance.

Joe glimpsed a body lying in the dust where Heywood had stood . . . dead or alive, he could not tell.

Farther up the street, someone fired a rifle from around a corner. Yet farther north, another marksman boomed out shot after shot. These last two guns were enough to keep the remnants of the Milstead gang pinned down.

Joe realized that there had also been sporadic pistol fire inside the saloon, but the beer hall was now quiet. The U.S. marshal was nowhere in sight.

The Milsteads were returning fire from behind their scant cover, and Joe feared that they would break for their horses. There was a momentary lull in the shooting.

"Ev Milstead!" Joe yelled. "It's Joe Trento. We've got half a dozen men out here . . . you're surrounded! Stop shooting and throw out your guns!"

There was a short silence, then, "You're crazy, Trento! You're the cause of all this. You think we'd surrender to you?"

Joe called back, "You've got two dead brothers already! Think of your pa . . . and your sister."

"Mind your own damn business, Trento! I can take care of my kin. We've got plenty of guns on our side, too . . . you and whoever you have with you best ride out. We've got the law on our side—you're a wanted man!"

"You're a fool, Milstead! There's a federal marshal who's seen everything, and I've got men up the street, besides myself—"

"And one over here," called out Thaddeus Corbett. "I'd recommend that you boys heed Joe's advice . . . I could put a bullet in each of your backs right now." The voice spoke mysteriously out of the dark. "The marshal is in the saloon: he's hit, but he'll live. He's seen and heard everything. Now, we've got you penned in—it won't take much to drop the bunch of you, and in case you're wondering, your cardplayin' partners are either dead or a mile out of town by now."

The moon was high over the town, and Joe could see almost as well as in daylight. Ev called out again, "My boys will be back! They'll be a dozen men ridin' into town by daylight! You sons of bitches better throw out the guns, not us!"

"You deaf as well as stupid, Milstead?" yelled Joe. "You heard the man—we could cut you down right now, and daylight is six hours away."

There was no reply to this, save some low grumblings as Ev's men discussed things among themselves. That they were at an extreme disadvantage was obvious. In a moment a voice shouted, "Hold your fire, we're comin' out!"

Joe's heart leapt with joy, only to sink a second later.

"Everybody freeze! Ev, goddamnit, it's Spence! Don't give in to these bastards! I've got my gun on Trento right now!"

Joe looked slowly over his shoulder. Behind him was a narrow passageway between two buildings—not much more than a crack. In it, about ten feet down, stood a wounded Spence Milstead, rifle trained on Joe.

"I want everyone to hold their fire," shouted Spence. "If you men with Joe Trento shoot at my boys, Trento here'll die!"

Spence Milstead had been hit in the shoulder by the shot from across the street. Joe surmised that the big man had fallen off the rear of the building, regained consciousness, and snuck up the alley. The street was quiet. Joe prayed that everyone would hesitate long enough. He knew that he had to take Spence. If not, the Milsteads would kill them all.

"Give it up, Milstead!" Joe called. "You shoot me and your clan'll be wiped out. I've got half a dozen men in town," Joe lied.

"Shut up and toss your guns into the street," replied Spence. "And get them a ways out there."

Joe was in a nearly helpless position, belly down, and lying under a wagon. He laid the Winchester in front of him and gave it a shove. It came to rest, covered with dust, out in the middle of Main Street.

"Now the six-guns," commanded Spence. "No tricks."

Joe hoped that the shadows under the wagon would save him. He moved his hands slowly toward his holsters, then rolled swiftly once, twice, three times, deeper into the shadows away from Spence.

A shot cracked and a puff of dirt jumped a foot from Joe, who was on his back with his own guns out. The two revolvers roared, and Spence Milstead fell for the second time that night. This time he would not rise.

Slowly Joe got to his feet. A shadow rushed toward him, and Joe almost shot before recognizing Corbett. Corbett trotted up and clapped Joe on the back with a sigh of relief. They stared down at Spence and the growing pool of blood in the dirt.

"Let's round up the others," Joe said, after a moment.

Ev Milstead was the only one of the family left, and he had a bad arm. When he heard Joe and Thad call out that Spence was down, he knew that they had lost.

"We've had it, boys," he said to his companions. "No sense all of us dying tonight." He called out to the street for a second time, "Hold your fire, we're comin' out!"

Ev, Chico, and two cowhands Joe had seen at the burnt slope, drifted out into the street, hands overhead. José Valero appeared, rifle at the ready. Grundy was helping Heywood to his feet.

A dozen townsfolk appeared and Joe called out instructions. "Someone get inside and tend to the marshal. Thad, maybe you can show these folks where he is. Somebody else get the doctor, if he's not already here. Let's see who all's been hit." Joe felt somehow that this was his mess, and that he should take charge.

Corbett had removed the weapons from Ev and his companions and now walked toward the Red Dawn, followed by several men. The doctor, carrying a medical bag, trotted after them. Joe bent over Fergus to check for a pulse.

"Dead," he announced. "José, escort these fellows over to the jailhouse. Looks like the deputy will be over in a minute." Sure enough, Grundy was helping Billy Heywood slowly across the street.

There was a pinkish glow in the eastern sky by the time everything was cleaned up and everyone tended to. Inside the saloon, there was another wounded man besides Keyes and one dead, both local gun toughs and gamblers.

Jack Keyes was taken to his room in the hotel and tended to by Doc Steinhauser. He'd been belly shot, an ugly, painful wound, but he'd live. He had regained consciousness briefly before falling into a deep sleep.

Heywood's wound was less serious, although a bullet was lodged in his shoulder. He was up and around. Joe, Corbett, and Valero crowded into the little jailhouse along with Heywood, and watched as Al Grundy stoked the small stove in order to make coffee. The four prisoners sulked in the cell that had held Joe Trento not long ago.

"Can't believe it," remarked Billy Heywood. "That marshal steppin' up at the last second and all, and Fergus lettin' go at me anyway."

"It was a long shot for him," said Joe, "but I reckon he saw no other way out. Likely, he figured it was only you two lawmen against his whole clan."

"I reckon," agreed Heywood. "I never figured to see you again, Trento, and here you show up with a small army! Say, that reminds me, you busted out of jail. By rights, I oughta lock you up, too!" The deputy looked concerned.

"Partner," said Joe, "there's only one hoosegow in this town, and I'd be obliged not to share it with its current occupants. Besides, as soon as you're fit to ride, I can show you proof that will clear me of that killing."

Everyone in the little room, including the prisoners, looked at Joe in surprise, for he had told no one about the body.

"I found the body," Joe said, "and it's miles from the place where I was run down, and it's not buried like old Cal said it was. The truth'll be obvious enough when you see it."

"What do you figure happened to him?" asked Corbett.

"I'll leave that to the law to decide," said Joe, "but, of course, someone killed the fellow, and there just isn't a big population around these parts, if you know what I mean."

"You son of a bitch!" growled Ev Milstead from the cell. "Don't go a layin' that killin' on us! Why the hell would we kill our own man?"

"I'm not sayin' you did or you didn't," replied Joe. "I'm just sayin' he's dead, and I can pretty well clear myself of it. Why would anyone kill 'im? Maybe he was interested in one of your womenfolk and one of you didn't like it . . . I've a notion he and Millie might've been sweet on each other. But like I said, that'll be for the law to decide."

"That's the biggest pile of crap I've ever heard," snarled Ev.

"Trento, I still don't know about you goin' free just now," said Heywood. "The main thing old Cal and the boys had folks riled up about was you escapin' like you did and not bein' tracked down. It won't look good, you walking around free."

"Tell you what, partner," said Joe, "I'll stay put right here till Marshal Keyes has his wits about him. We'll tell him the whole story and he can either arrest me or let me go."

"I'd appreciate that, Joe."

"Just remember, I busted out after Josh Parker was shot dead and that mob was after me, and you were miles out of town. Make sure you mention that to Keyes!"

"That's right, goddamnit!" burst in Al Grundy. He straightened up from his work over the stove. "Can't expect a man t' sit still fer a lynchin', especially if there ain't no law about to stick up fer 'im!"

Heywood nodded thoughtfully as he contemplated this.

"Speakin' of Keyes," said Corbett, "I believe I'll mosey down and check in on him. There's really no one to look after him, him bein' a stranger and all, and doc's prob'ly itchin' to get back home to bed."

Corbett left, and Heywood stared after him a moment. Then he looked over at José Valero, who was leaning quietly in a corner. He noted the tough-looking Mexican's trail-worn clothes and gear.

"If I didn't know you some, Joe," said the deputy, "I'd lay money that this group of yours are outlaws themselves! You've sure got the looks, anyway."

Joe grinned—for the first time in days—realizing that Heywood knew nothing about his wild-looking companions. "Don't fret over it," Joe said. "None of us is a wanted man, 'cept me, I guess. Corbett and Valero here are respected citizens down Morelos way."

"Ha!" blurted out Al. "Thad Corbett is about as respectable as a rattlesnake. True, he ain't wanted, but that's only because he's sly as a fox, too."

Heywood looked at the three grinning men, not knowing what to think.

A shot rang out, then another, and the men jumped toward the door. Joe reached it first and bounded into the street. His heart froze, as the early dawn revealed the body of Thaddeus Corbett, lying on the ground, about halfway to the hotel.

CHAPTER 20

JOE'S EYES SEARCHED up and down Main Street until he saw the figure of a man, a big man, way up by the livery. He was moving swiftly between two buildings and out of sight.

Grundy and Valero dashed past Joe, heading for Corbett. Joe took off at a run, sprinting toward the livery. He cut down an alley and arrived at the edge of the desert in time to see two men on horseback galloping off to the southwest.

Joe now raced south, behind the buildings of Main Street, weaving through a maze of outhouses and shacks. The big man had worn the garb of a Mexican desperado. It could only be one thing—some of Deligro's gang had come after Corbett. Maybe after me too, Joe thought.

He reached the place where he had tied Blue earlier that evening. He leapt into the saddle and spurred the startled horse into a fast gallop, heading in the same direction as the fleeing men—the men who, he thought sickly, had probably just put Thad Corbett in his grave.

The tall blue roan stretched himself out over the desert floor in response to Joe's urgings. The horse had been pushed hard recently, and Joe kept this in mind as he planned his course of action.

He would top a small rise in a minute. If the bandits were still in sight, he would continue the chase, hoping to eventually run them down—a long and grueling prospect—or at least get close enough for a few shots. If the pair was not in sight, then Joe would have to pick up their trail and follow it, another kind of grueling task.

He topped the rise and was met by a brilliant display of

pink and orange sunrise, bursting over the eastern horizon. He squinted and scanned the country ahead.

Nothing. The two cutthroats had either disappeared into the rolling terrain, or their distant forms were hidden by the glare of the sun.

Perhaps it was best. Although Blue was a strong, well-muscled gelding, he had been worked almost constantly over the past few weeks. The outlaw ponies, by contrast, may have had several days of rest and good feed. They might easily pull away in a long, fast run.

Presently, the Mexicans might not even realize that they were being pursued. If Joe was cautious, he might be able to travel at his own pace and make the decisions concerning how, when, and where to confront the pair.

Joe trotted down the slope so as not to be as visible from a distance. He worked his way northward, looking for the tracks of two fast-moving horses. It was slow work. He had to hold Blue to a walk, and he dismounted frequently in order to search the ground more closely.

A half hour passed, and Joe had still not found the trail that he'd expected to be obvious. He assumed that he had topped the rise south of the Mexicans' trail, and so he'd searched northward. Could this have been a mistake? Perhaps the bandits, for whatever reason, had traveled sharply southward for a spell, before heading southwestward again.

Joe dismounted and led Blue southward, eyeing the sandy ground closely. It was hot now, the sun having turned to a white, blazing globe. Sweat ran into Joe's eyes, and he paused to wipe his face.

Then he saw it. The tracks of two horses, coming over the rise at a canter. They disappeared into the ocotillo and mesquite to the southwest.

They would not return home through Maysville, which was due south and the usual route. These two seemed to be planning to go as the crow flies, riding straight across

hundreds of miles of parched basins and rugged mountains.

Joe felt a twinge of excitement as he mounted up and
followed the trail at a walk. He held in check his desire to
hurry—for two reasons. First, he did not want to lose sight
of the tracks in the sandy soil. Second, he was wary of
overtaking the duo unexpectedly.

Joe was counting on the fugitives not suspecting close
pursuit and therefore not watching their backtrail. If they
were in no hurry, they'd probably even stop at night, while
Joe would not. He would instead spur Blue into a slow
canter for several miles at a time, but only after the sun
went down and the cool breezes had begun.

The day wore on, and horse and rider sweated and grew
weary. The sun beat down on the scorched land, and Joe
continued at a walk. The heat discouraged a faster gait, as
did the fear of raising dust. Joe constantly scanned the
horizon for sign of the fugitives, but he saw nothing.

He knew there were mountains coming up to the west.
They would become larger and more defined as the day
passed. Eventually, the outlaws' trail would lead through a
portion of those rugged crags, then into more desert
beyond.

Would that be a time to make a move? Joe had noticed
long ago that the tracks he followed had slowed to those of
walking horses. He stopped and dismounted for a closer
look.

Fresh . . . very fresh . . . but how far ahead? One hour?
Two? It was impossible to say.

Joe considered the risks. The Mexicans might know that
he was following, in which case they could wait in ambush.
Or, if both he and the fugitives topped separate rises at
the same instant, they might suddenly become plainly
visible to each other, resulting in a long-distance shooting
match or an all-out chase. Finally, and most likely, when

Joe picked up the pace after dusk, he risked riding right into the outlaws' camp as they stopped for the night. Ideally, Joe would guess when to slow down and thereby approach the sleeping outlaws quietly.

The sun was well past its zenith by now, and Joe began thinking about water. There was very little in the canteen he carried, for he had departed the ranch in haste yesterday, hurrying to Heywood's aid and had not expected to venture into the desert. The outlaws, no doubt, had planned for a hard, dry trek. They most likely carried enough water to even provide their mounts with a few swallows. Perhaps they would not be seeking out a drinking place after all . . . no chance for Joe to anticipate a distant watering hole and beat them to it, and not much hope of passing a watering hole for himself.

He and Blue would have to keep following for as long as they could. With some luck, they might cross a stream or pass a spring after entering the mountains that evening.

They passed through a sparse forest of tall agave, and around clusters of ocotillo. Joe thought of the moist, edible fruit that the latter plant produced, but was not yet thirsty enough to stop and taste it.

He checked his guns as he rode. The Winchester seemed to be fine despite its slide through the dusty street. He had already checked the pistols and reloaded the chambers spent on Spence Milstead.

Slowly, the gray mountains loomed closer, and the land became broken and rough. They were climbing into the hills now, and still no glimpse of the fugitives.

The trail rose through a dry wash, which was apparently visited by larger quantities of water than the surrounding terrain, for throughout the arroyo were patches of grass, mostly dry and brown, but still green in one place. Joe stopped at the latter spot and dismounted, dropping the reins. The horses immediately fell to cropping the dry forage.

The outlaws had also stopped briefly at this place, and hoofprints were abundant. Joe swallowed what little water there was in his canteen, then squatted to examine the ground.

The tracks were new, of course, but exactly how new could not be discerned. He had seen Indian scouts accurately predict very small differences in age from such sign, but he himself could not.

His nose, however, told him of something his eyes had missed, and a few steps away he found the fresh droppings of one of the Mexican ponies. These he could read more easily. Still fresh and moist in the middle, dry and hard on the surface. Joe frowned. He guessed at least one, probably two hours old. He remembered the time he had squandered trying to locate the trail on the rise outside town. No doubt the bandits had increased their lead considerably while he had searched.

Joe was feeling weary—the effects of a night without sleep and a long ride with no food and little water. He would have liked to remain in the little arroyo and rest awhile, maybe dig for water. Would he be able to follow the trail, in the dark, at a sufficient pace to overtake the duo before daybreak? Joe reluctantly got to his feet and mounted up again. These two must not get away after what they had done.

The sun was low behind them as horse and rider climbed into the hills. No longer afraid of being spotted, Joe quickened the pace. He trotted and cantered for short distances whenever the terrain permitted. The hills were not as broken and rock-strewn as those around Morelos; these were similar to the mountainous forms surrounding Joe's ranch, only less densely forested.

As darkness fell, he noticed that the trail led toward a low saddle in the mountain range. He smiled to himself. This fact, together with his knowledge of the outlaws' general direction, would allow him to proceed more rapidly through the dark night, unhindered by frequent stops to read the trail. The fugitives were almost certainly headed for the saddle.

Joe figured the pair would stop shortly after dark. He had put Blue into an easy lope up a grassy incline, but now reined in to a walk. He decided to allow the Mexicans plenty of time to drift off to sleep.

Joe was even contemplating another rest himself, when he noticed Blue's ears flicking backward with uncommon frequency. He turned casually to check his backtrail, and his eyes met with a nightmarish scene.

CHAPTER 21

JOE TRENTO STARED in horror through the soft moonlight. A half dozen horsemen had burst out of the mesquite thickets and were racing silently toward him! He could see in an instant that they were naked men—not Mexicans— with long, straight hair and smooth faces. Joe detected the forms of a short bow and a long, feathered lance. Apaches!

He had neglected to concern himself with the threat of Indian attack, such were the other matters weighing upon his mind. He had ridden noisily and carelessly; now he had been detected.

A rifle cracked and a shot whistled by in the dark. In a flash, Joe dropped the reins and pulled the Colts. The pistols roared and he spurred the prancing roan. Blue took off like a greyhound, and Joe grabbed a handful of mane in order to hang on.

The weary cowboy hauled the reins to the right and touched his spurs to the horse again. Blue cut hard in the new direction as two arrows flew over his rump. Then another shot, and Joe felt an impact against his right calf, as though clubbed with a steel bar.

Joe had detected the attack soon enough to have a fighting chance. He covered the remainder of the open meadow and crashed into the brush at its upper end. He urged the gelding onward and the animal lunged wildly, leaping up the mountainside in huge strides as branches cut and lashed viciously at Joe's face.

He wondered how long his mount could continue such exertion. He heard the Indian ponies crashing through

159

behind him, then he was on open hillside again, and running—a labored, gasping gallop.

Only seconds had passed since the attack had commenced, and Joe had had no time to think. He knew instinctively, however, that he could not continue to run; he must turn and fight—soon. Just then the land fell away into a rocky depression—a streambed at times—and Joe whispered a short prayer of thanks. He hauled the horse to a stop, grabbed the rifle from its boot, and jumped to the ground.

Joe scrambled to the top of the gully and flopped down. He focused and listened, and made out five riders galloping toward him. There had been six—had he gotten one with the Colts?

He aimed and levered off three shots. Two Indians fell backward, and a third leapt to the ground as his horse went down, hit the ground running, and quickly leapt onto one of the free ponies who had yet to break stride. The three mounted warriors then whirled without hesitation and raced back downhill, leaving their companions behind. Joe fired twice more, but missed.

That meant three Apaches still alive, maybe more. Within minutes, they could have him pinned down. Joe slid down to the gelding, which stood with head low, gasping for air.

"Sorry, old buddy," he whispered, "we gotta run for it again."

He peered up the mountainside in the direction of the pass. The clearing ended about fifty yards up. Joe mounted and urged Blue out of the creek bed and into a slow canter, which was all the spent animal could muster. They made the thicket without sign of the Indians, and Joe breathed a sigh of relief.

He hoped the Apaches would give up. They'd have wounded to tend to, most likely, and some would have to ride double or walk or be left behind.

Joe let Blue pick his way slowly through the trees and scrub, as the animal was almost completely spent. Besides a faster gait would be too noisy, and Joe preferred that his whereabouts remain obscure.

Joe's senses were strained to their limits. His ears now listened for sounds of stalking Indians as well as indications of the Mexicans ahead. His eyes searched for firelight and unusual shapes in the dark, both ahead and behind. His nose sniffed for wood smoke.

The bullet in his leg began to burn like a hot brand. Joe had previously feared that he would grow drowsy; perhaps the pain would keep him awake. Suddenly the soft earth and pine needles that had covered the ground for the past mile gave way to another rocky gully, and this time Joe heard the trickle of a stream. Blue also sensed the presence of water, and Joe had to restrain the animal from lunging wildly down the embankment.

Both horse and rider drank deeply and quietly under the soft starlight. After a time, Blue moved off to investigate the short grass growing nearby. Joe turned to his wound. He was able to remove his boot, but had to tear the pant leg to get at the spot.

The bullet bulged, white and grotesque, just beneath the surface of the skin. It could have been a lot worse, he thought. He drew his knife. Squeezing the bullet between thumb and forefinger, he made a quick slice, then worked the slug out of the wound.

Joe let the wound bleed freely for a moment, then clamped a hand over it and hobbled to the stream. He stood in the shallow water and bathed the gash as best he could, then bound it tightly with a strip of cloth torn from his shirttail. It felt better, bound up and with the slug removed.

He heard the sound of a scraping boot, and his head jerked up. There, on the opposite bank, grinning wolfishly, stood the fat Mexican, and next to him, his scrawny friend. Both had gun barrels leveled.

"Do not worry about Indians no more," said the fat one. "Raul and me will scare them away." The two bandits laughed.

"Watch him, Raul," continued Deligro, "he is a slippery one. I think he was with Corbett last week." Deligro sloshed over to Joe. "Maybe you the one who get my brother, eh?"

Joe could think of nothing to say, so he just stood. He experienced an unusual, eerie sensation in his gut as he gazed through the dimness, listening to the threatening voice. He couldn't lie his way out of this one—they recognized him, and it was obvious he had come after them. Upon hearing the Indian attack, they must have doubled back to see what was going on.

"You don't answer . . . then maybe you are the one!" Deligro moved swiftly forward and struck hard with an uppercut, catching Joe under the chin. Joe blacked out for an instant and stumbled back against the bank. When he looked again, the outlaw was walking toward Blue in order to pilfer Joe's gear, too greedy to wait until later.

They would beat him to a pulp, no doubt, then shoot him in the head. Well, thought Joe, he would not permit them so much pleasure. He would go for the Colts, and no doubt the skinny one would cut him down, but he would end it his way.

Just then a twig snapped loudly, and the three turned. A voice called out in Spanish from the brush downhill. Joe recognized Valero's voice. He looked to see the Mexicans' reaction. The big one muttered something softly to the other, then crouched and began to move rapidly upstream, keeping to what cover there was. Raul kept his rifle trained on Joe.

"Joe, get your horse!" Valero shouted. "He knows I will kill him if he shoots."

It was possible he would get away without anyone being killed. But very unlikely, Joe thought.

The skinny one stood petrified, realizing the deadly situation he now faced. But what about Deligro? Suddenly, Joe realized that Valero must not have seen the big man!

"José, there's another one—upstream—about twenty yards!" Joe peered through the dim light, straining to keep sight of the bandit.

Upon hearing the warning, Deligro hesitated, then swung around and aimed his rifle at Joe! The shot whizzed by him.

Valero, seeing what had to be done, cut down Raul Sanchez. Joe dove onto his belly, guns out and smoking. His leg burned with pain.

Three more shots were fired by Deligro in rapid succession. Joe's leap had caught the renegade off guard, and now he began to panic. He'd seen Raul go down; he could not see Joe. He levered off two more rounds and began backing away.

Joe gambled that the time was right. He jumped up and half ran, half hobbled along the mud of the creek bed. When he guessed that he was about even with Deligro's last position, he turned and leapt up the embankment, crashing through the brush, guns held level at his hips.

The Mexican heard the sound of Joe's reckless pursuit, and he knew he could not escape the younger, faster man. The outlaw ponies were another fifty yards off. With a growl, Deligro whirled, tossing the rifle away, going for his pistols instead.

Joe burst through a bunch of dry ocotillo in time to see the last half of Deligro's draw. Again he leaped, the sound of gunfire in his ears, blinding muzzle blasts ahead. Hot lead seared his shoulder, and his own guns roared. He hit the ground and rolled, then fired again.

All was quiet, and Joe could see nothing but a cloud of blue smoke. He slid slowly back down to the creek bed and crouched there. Still nothing. Making his way cautiously downstream, he found the welcome sight of Valero squatting by a small, still form.

"Dead?"

"Yes. The other?"

"Not sure. We'd best keep low."

Together the two spread out and worked their way through the tangled brush.

"Here, *amigo*," Valero called at last. Joe walked over and observed the body of Felipe Deligro lying spread-eagled on the ground, a bullet through his chest and one through his throat.

Dawn was approaching as the two men finished scooping a shallow grave and covering the two bodies with stones. Valero did most of the work and insisted at one point that Joe stop and rest his leg. The wound, as a result of the recent activity, had continued bleeding through the makeshift bandages. Valero, who'd had some experience at these things, built a small fire and boiled water. He disappeared into the forest and returned ten minutes later with large handfuls of vegetation, which he boiled and used to dress the wound.

Valero had ample provisions in his saddlebags, and the two took time to eat and drink.

"Never reckoned any of you would come after me," Joe commented. "Figured I was on my own."

"We did not think you would go after them alone," said Valero. "We expected you to find the trail, then return to town."

"They'd be through that pass by now if I had. No tellin' if the trail would've held out."

Valero nodded.

Joe hesitated, then spoke. "Corbett . . . is he—"

"Alive," said Valero. "He will need much time to become the same again, but he is alive."

Joe's face broke into a wide grin, which Valero returned. The two sat in silence. A kangaroo rat scurried by in the brush, finishing up its nocturnal business. A kit fox passed, pausing to stare at the unexpected campfire, then melting away.

"The marshal, Jack Keyes, is better, too," Valero said finally. "Heywood told him about the body you found. Keyes says if it's true, you will be free of the murder charge."

Joe nodded. Everything was going to work out, and none of them killed. He felt that he should jump up and shout with joy, but instead, he simply sat in numb disbelief. He felt good, certainly, but somehow it all did not seem right—all the fighting and killing.

"Something else," continued José. "The boy from Maysville—Pablo. He rode in with the body of the old Milstead . . . Cal, I think." Joe looked up, his expression a mixture of surprise and concern. "Seems that Cal Milstead talked this other man—Walker was his name—into going with him to track you. They got to Maysville and heard that you were friendly with the Mexicans there. They started to get rough, trying to get information. Pablo ended up gunning the old man down. Walker jumped on a horse and rode out."

Joe remembered Pablo and the shotgun they had put in his hands. Had that been right? Then he remembered something Corbett had said. Something about the type of men who had come west so far, and about the people still to come. Men with families, businesses, and dreams. That was why they had to fight . . . not just for themselves, but for the others . . . folks like Pablo and Lupita . . . Sean Colin . . . Carter Andersen and Van Brooks.

Joe thought of all this, and of an abandoned prospector's shack in a canyon miles to the north. Little by little, he felt better. It was over. He began to feel very good.

A pink sun was climbing above the mountains behind

them as Joe Trento and José Valero trotted down the open desert. Their talk turned briefly to the ranch and the work ahead. Joe had forgotten the excitement and energy that the challenge of becoming a successful stockman had previously brought to him. Now that he was no longer chasing or being chased, fighting or hiding, these feelings returned. Valero was infected too, and as he offered his ideas and proposals, Joe's zeal was augmented even further. Much to do, but a wealth of land to use.

After a mile or so, Joe began to glance northward, toward the distant outline of the mountains that sheltered his land. He reined up abruptly.

"José, will you ride into town and report what happened? And lend me a canteen, will you?"

Valero looked astonished. "Why?"

Joe grabbed the canteen that was passed over and took up his reins. "I have to tell Elizabeth and Millie what happened. It won't be easy, especially for Millie. But I'd rather they hear it from me."

"You sure, Joe Trento?" asked Valero.

"I'm sure," Joe replied, as the big blue turned away and broke into an easy lope. It was still cool enough to make some time. With any luck he would be at the prospector's shack by nightfall.

If you have enjoyed this book and would like to receive details on other Walker Western titles, please write to:

Western Editor
Walker and Company
435 Hudson Street
New York, NY 10014